DOMESTIC DISCIPLINE

FOR DANIEL

(Extended All Fem-Dom Edition)

by Mistress Jade

(with Mark Maguire)

Published by

markmaguirebooks.co.uk

"If baby I'm the bottom,
You're the Top!"

Cole Porter

CONTENTS

INTRODUCTION

The house was different from all the rest. There was certainly something about it, clearly standing out from all the others in Station Road. Now there's a misnomer. Station Road hasn't led to a station for more than 50 years, yet that's still the name of the main road through our village. But I'm jumping ahead. This is all about the first time I walked down Station Road five years ago, when I first moved here.

All the houses were smart, certainly, but number 76 was more than that. It had an almost disciplined look about it, as though the owner was a stickler for detail. How true that was going to turn out to be!

My name is Daniel. I'm 31 now, and I was just 26 when I moved here to Little Lavenham. I suppose you could say I'd gone off the rails in quite a big way while I'd been living in London. I'd had quite a good job, working in a small retailer selling upmarket deli foods. The pay was quite good but I just took it as my right without giving anything back in return. I whiled away the hours, bored out of my wits, waiting for each day to end.

Then I'd go out on the town getting drunk, with no thought at all for my long-suffering wife and child at home. I got involved in the wrong things, mixed with the wrong crowd....and finally lost my despairing, lovely young wife in the process.

My drunken outbursts had become more and more frequent until one day I hit out at her. She hadn't done anything wrong. She'd merely criticised me for my complete lack of responsibility when it came to helping with anything around the house and, most importantly, looking after our young daughter.

I hit her hard – and that was the end.

"I want a divorce" was all she'd said.

And now, here I was, trying to make a new start and put an end to my old ways of selfishness and thoughtlessness.

What has all this to do with me spotting that highly immaculate house at number 76 Station Road? Well, when I tell you the owner turned out to be an ex-headmistress of the "old school" type, you may be able to guess.

She has completely changed my life and put me back on the straight and narrow. I am so grateful to her and I will tell anybody so. What I don't generally tell people is HOW she has done that. You see, I now regularly visit a highly respected, very experienced adult disciplinarian and mistress.

Olivia is 46, and she's been dishing out realistic and very painful spankings, canings and other imaginative discipline to deserving men for well over twenty years. There's not much that she doesn't know about adult corporal punishment.

When I've behaved badly or made a mistake, I receive embarrassing bare-bottom spankings, hard paddlings and slipperings, corner time, mouth soapings and line writing – depending on how bad I've been.

As you may have guessed, the ultimate sanction is the cane, although Olivia does have a birch which she brings out if she decides she wants to really drive a message home.

When I have completely screwed up big time, I know I'm going to suffer under the relentless onslaught of Olivia's hard wooden hairbrush being vigorously applied to my soft, receptive bare buttocks – and I can tell you that hairbrush absolutely hurts like hell.

The pain builds increasingly until I am reduced to begging and pleading for it to stop.... but this is where Olivia is such a superb disciplinarian. She never takes any notice of my pleading and just carries on with even more enthusiasm until SHE decides to finish.

Then, if it's been a really major mistake I've made, there'll be a reminder that I've still got the cane to come, and I am sent to the corner to wait, hands on head.

Why, oh why do I keep returning to Olivia, again and again?

You'll find out as you read what follows. You'll read my account of how I met her, how I learned to cope with the painful effects of her favourite, flexible punishment cane, and how I discovered the tremendous benefits of completely submitting to her adult discipline regime.

I'm a different person now, as I said. My arse is different too, as it's frequently covered in furiously burning stripes produced by her expert canings. My bottom is no longer mine. It's hers... and I'm often reminded of that whenever I sit down.

So here goes. I'll tell you about her expert punishment techniques, and explain why she's probably the best user of the cane there's ever been.

CHAPTER ONE – MY BIG MISTAKE

I'd only been a week at Little Lavenham when I noticed the postcard in the window of the village shop.

"Part-time assistant required. Apply within."

My small rented flat was going to have to be paid for, and I knew I had the experience needed. I had a reference from the deli where I'd worked in London (which, to tell you the truth, had been rather more complimentary than I'd deserved as the owner had been pleased to get rid of me) and during my short interview I was able to demonstrate that I knew about dealing with stock, making sales and handling cash.

To cut a long story short, the shop keeper didn't need a lot of persuading and I soon had the job.

"Could do with some new blood around here," he'd said. "Everyone else has lived here for ages. You're new. You could bring in some new business."

I was to work alongside another young assistant who had been there several years. A slim, 21-year-old, dark haired girl by the name of Laura, she was pretty, smart and efficient. She worked hard every day and whenever there was a lull or a coffee break, she would take the opportunity to boast to me about her prowess with the young men of the village. Rubbing my nose in it, she made it clear that she was better than me in more or less every respect.

If only I'd learned the lessons I should have learned in London. I could have turned over a new leaf and done just what the shopkeeper said. I didn't, however. I lazed around through the day and never gave much attention to the customers who seemed an unwelcome distraction to me.

The small shop was rather cluttered as a result of attempting to sell just about everything that could be called a basic need in the village. The nearest big town was more than ten miles away, so we did a big trade in milk, bread, newspapers, wine and toilet rolls.

I made my home behind the old-fashioned wooden counter where I could usually be found perched on a stool in a corner, doing my best to avert my gaze from engaging with the steady stream of customers who arrived throughout the day.

My fellow assistant Laura was usually the one who served them. I have to admit I regarded her with some degree of contempt as she hurried around at their beck and call. Rather her than me, I thought!

On a particular Tuesday afternoon, which turned out to be memorable for a number of reasons, it was pouring with rain outside. The small shop was darker than usual and the atmosphere was gloomy generally. I was engrossed in my smartphone when someone said "How much are these potatoes?"

I looked up to see a rather foreboding figure peering at me over the top of her glasses. She rested one of her elbows on the counter as she spoke. Her outfit was smart, neat and sexy, with a red open necked blouse and dark brown closely fitting skirt. A strong-looking woman, she had an air of authority about her right from the start.

"Sorry?" I said nonchalantly, looking down again at my phone.

"You SHOULD be sorry!" she snapped. "I've just asked you the price of the potatoes and you don't look as though you could give a damn about either the potatoes or me!"

"How should I know?" I countered. "Are they not marked?"

"Marked?" she repeated loudly. She bristled with rage and rose to her full height as she said "I know what SHOULD be marked, young man.... your backside. If a young man had spoken to one of his elders like that when I was your age, he'd have got the cane."

I didn't subscribe to the notion of "elders" and I certainly had no fear of the cane. Its use had long been discontinued, and throughout my schooldays we'd all been able to be as rude as we liked to our teachers without the threat of any sanctions at all.

"The cane?" I laughed.

"Yes!" the customer stated categorically, turning bright red with anger as she continued "In my day, the cane was frequently used across the backsides of arrogant and insolent young men like you. An excellent way to teach a young man a memorable and very painful lesson. Its excruciating sting is not quickly forgotten."

"Calm down, can't you?" I responded with a grin. "Don't get your knickers in a twist!"

"Calm down?" she thundered. "And you've just referred to my knickers? Where is the manager?"

Laura had said nothing at all during this heated altercation, but now she spoke, almost enthusiastically.

"I'll get him," she said helpfully.

To summarise as quickly as I can, my boss was far from pleased, and at the end of a very heated and embarrassing conversation, I was allowed to keep my job and given a final warning. The irate customer was offered a complimentary hamper as an apology ... and I was to deliver it personally that evening.

Six o'clock came, and with it the end of my shift. I was firmly instructed to take the gift to the powerful-looking woman who had been so insulted by my rudeness, and to be extremely polite when I handed it to her.

Laura was amused, to say the least.

"Going to say sorry?" she smirked. "Going to admit you were a naughty young man?"

I didn't reply. As you can guess, I wasn't looking forward to meeting the customer again. Armed with the address, I set off to walk the length of the village, carrying the wicker basket filled with goodies which was to be the "making amends" gift.

Imagine my surprise when I found myself at the house I'd always noticed. The one I regarded as different from the rest.

I eased open the front gate and walked up the immaculately swept path, between two perfectly manicured lawns.

On reaching the porch, I was admiring the two colourful hanging baskets each side of the dark green front door when my eyes fell upon a small hand-written notice pinned on the doorframe.

"No hawkers, no free newspapers, no charity collectors."

I wondered if I could be classified as a hawker but assured myself that my visit was expected and that I was the bearer of a gift in any case. I rang the bell.

"Ah! My insolent and rude young friend!"

The householder's remark on opening the door to me was hardly welcoming. I remembered my strict instructions to be polite so made no response other than to smile slightly as I thrust the hamper into her hands.

"You've brought me a gift? How kind!"

She took the present and turned indoors to place it on the small table just visible in the hallway. Like the garden, it was neat and tidy. I could see heavily flocked wallpaper, a mirror and an umbrella stand. At the far end of the corridor I could see a grandfather clock.

"Have you nothing to say?" she inquired.

"Er … I'm sorry for being rude … er, Miss," I stammered.

"Mmmmmm." She didn't seem particularly impressed. "I suppose you're calling me Miss as you don't know my name," he added. "Well it's Hamilton. Olivia Hamilton. And yours is ……?"

"Daniel," I replied. "Daniel Cornish."

"And are you?" Olivia snapped.

"Am I what?"

"Are you Cornish, damn you!"

She was growing angry again now and I didn't want that.

"No Miss. I don't think so. I guess someone in my family history was originally, but it's just a surname. Quite an unusual one I think."

There! I'd done it. I'd started to be pleasantly conversational with this difficult woman who had begun to stare right through me.

"You're new here, aren't you?" she went on. "Where have you come from?"

"London, Miss," I said more confidently. "I've only lived here a few weeks. I've got a little flat at the other end of the village. Well, I'm renting it. Nothing like this, though. Your house is so smart and your garden is amazing."

"Thank you," the woman replied, more warmly. "So … a new arrival. I suppose I should ask you in. Make an effort to be sociable."

"That's very nice of you," I said.

I wasn't sure how I felt. I hadn't made any friends in the village so far as there seemed to be very few people of around my age. Now I was getting an offer from the very person I would have most liked to avoid.

Olivia Hamilton opened the door more widely. Light streamed into the previously rather dingy hallway. "Come along in," she invited.

Then, as I stepped inside, I saw the thing that was to change my life. Sticking up proudly from the umbrella stand near the door was a slender, crook-handled school cane.

CHAPTER TWO – COMPOUNDING THE ERROR

Ten minutes later and we were sitting comfortably in her lounge. She'd made coffee and brought it in on a tray bearing a steaming cafetiere along with elegant bone china cups and saucers. I could see immediately that Olivia did everything with style.

I sank back into the sofa and adjusted the cushions to make myself more comfortable. My own coffee was always instant, drunk from a heavily stained mug emblazoned with the witty words "The Boss". If only I was! Not much chance of ever being that.

Self-image was not my thing. I suppose deep down inside I knew I was a waster. Behind my bravado, I was a nervous individual with very little confidence or belief in myself.

As the conversation developed, Olivia asked about my life so far, my family, my upbringing, etc. etc. I answered all her questions, but found myself getting emotional when it came to talking about how I'd lost my wife through my own stupid fault.

All the time, as we talked and talked, my thoughts returned to what I'd seen in the umbrella stand in the hall. I'd seen photos of such items before, but had never actually seen one for real. A school cane. I couldn't begin to imagine how much an implement like that could hurt, especially if applied with vigour. What was it doing there?

Her questions continued, and my answers became fuller. Nevertheless, I couldn't muster the confidence to ask HER anything so the conversation was rather one-sided. Eventually I summoned up the courage.

"And what about you?" I enquired. "What's your history? How long have you lived in the village?"

Olivia Hamilton looked pleased I'd eventually asked.

"I was educated at London University," she said. "I did my degree in history and then trained to teach. Eventually I became a Headmistress of a grammar school at Maidenhead. We had a high reputation, although I say it myself, and a sixth form which was the best in the country, going by our exam results."

"I see," was all I could manage to say. I just wasn't good at easy conversation – as Olivia was discovering!

"When I retired," she continued, "I came here to live and I fit in very well here. I like the pace of life. It suits me. I was lucky. I had a very good inheritance from my parents that enabled me to retire early. Very early. I'm only 46 so there's a great deal more vigour in me, as you can imagine. And being a divorcee, I have lots of time to myself for my own pursuits."

How full Olivia's answer was, I thought. How well she expressed herself. My thoughts turned back to that slender school cane I'd see in the hall. Why had she chosen to use the word vigour? Did she apply the cane with vigour to young men's backsides?

And would those backsides be bare?

I, Daniel Cornish, had been to a run-of-the-mill comprehensive school in Ealing, west London. I started to wish Olivia had been my Headmistress. Then I might have made something of myself.

We talked and talked. She made another cafetiere of coffee and brought in some shortbread.

The time seemed to pass more and more easily until, during a brief pause in the conversation, I heard the grandfather clock strike in the hall. It was nine o'clock and I'd been there since six!

I hadn't been home and I hadn't phoned my mother as I'd promised to do at seven. Worse still, I knew I should have gone on line to move some money into my current account.

Now I'd be charged a lot more interest on my overdraft which would eat in to my meagre resources even more than usual.

"Shit!" I cried out, without thinking. "I should have phoned my mother. And my fucking bank account will probably be frozen now. Bugger."

Mrs Hamilton's expression changed in an instant. Whereas she'd become quite friendly, still in a formal kind of way, now she was looking at me with a steely, icy gaze.

I'd relaxed so much in Olivia's company that I'd talked the way I usually did. All the evening so far I'd been careful how I'd said things. Even though she was only 46, she was so old-fashioned and so eloquently spoken that I felt I just had to watch my words.

Normally most of my sentences contained at least one swear word. It was how we'd all spoken when I was a teenager, and it had just continued.

None of my mates ever batted an eyelid as they all talked like that too, and our teachers had never dared to question our choice of expletives, being concerned about not seeming 'cool' themselves. They always acted as though they were our friends, rather than our educators.

"What did you just say, young man?"

I sat upright and leaned forward nervously.

"I'm really sorry, Olivia … er … I mean Miss …" I stammered.

"I didn't ask you whether or not you were sorry. I asked you what you had just said. Repeat it please, word for word."

I blushed bright red, remaining silent. I couldn't say it again in front of this stern foreboding woman.

"Repeat it! I'm waiting."

"Um … I said …… shit …" I whispered, almost inaudibly.

"Yes, you did. And the rest, please."

With great reluctance and embarrassment, I managed to whisper most of the remainder of my outburst, more or less correctly.

"I clearly remember what I said to you in the village store when you were rude to me there. Not as rude as you've just been now, I might add. How dare you speak to me like that!"

"I wasn't exactly speaking to you, Miss. I was sort of speaking to myself. Voicing my thoughts," I tried to explain.

"Your thoughts are filthy," she announced. "As I've just told you, I clearly remember what I said in the shop and I suspect you do too. Tell me what I said."

If it were possible, I would have turned even redder than I already was. Something inside me gave me the confidence to say quietly

"You said that if a young man had been as rude as that when you were young, he'd have got the cane … um … Miss."

My mind was racing ahead now as I pictured the vintage school cane I'd seen in the hall. It was so slender - elegant even - and obviously whippy. It certainly looked as though it could inflict a pretty painful, vicious sting. Surely, she couldn't be suggesting ...?

"Yes, the cane," she said, compounding my anxiety. "The perfect punishment."

I decided to try to deflect the conversation away from my latest mistake and ask about her own experience.

"Does a caning really hurt?" I asked lamely.

"Of course it bloody hurts!" she snorted. "That's the whole idea. A school cane is designed to hurt as much as possible. The flexibility, the thin diameter and the length make a unique combination that produces an absolutely intolerable, breath-taking sting."

I blushed bright red and looked at her nervously as she continued.

"Given in doses of six, the pain increases more and more with every stroke. Clever, don't you think? Particularly as it requires very little effort on the part of the giver. Just a determined flick of the wrist will produce a really powerful swipe that the recipient will remember for a very long time!"

I could hardly take all this in. Olivia spoke almost reverentially about this highly painful method of punishment.

I sat back fairly gingerly and managed to continue to keep the discussion away from me.

"So, you got caned yourself?" I asked. "When did it last happen, and what had you done wrong?"

I was quite fascinated now, and for some strange reason, so was my cock which had started to stir within my briefs. I hoped she wouldn't notice the increasing bulge as I placed my hands in my lap.

"My last caning was as a sixth former," she stated. "I'd failed for the third time to hand in an essay on the required date, and a third offence always meant a caning. It was the same for everyone – whether you were a young man or a young woman."

"You mean you were caned in the sixth form?" I asked, incredulously. "But surely you were 18 then?"

"Yes, of course. The Headmistress took the view – quite correctly as far as I'm concerned - that a caning would not be any less painful for a young adult. And the fact that she always caned on the bare meant that the embarrassment and humiliation were probably a bigger part of the punishment for a sixth former than the pain. It still bloody hurt though!"

I have to admit I was becoming hooked. The conversation was taking a much more intimate tone and I was more than intrigued as to how it was going to develop. I wanted to hear in full detail just what her sixth former caning had been like. The whole idea was really turning me on.

"Are you saying the Headmistress caned sixth form young men and women on their bare bottoms?"

"Yes, that's what I said and that's what she did."

"So, what happened exactly, if you went to the Headmistress to be caned?"

Olivia Hamilton remained silent for a moment and then began.

"I was eighteen, as I said, and I should have handed in my history essay on a particular Thursday morning. I was just a bit lazy, really. I couldn't get myself organised – and it was the third time I'd done it. I knew the cane was the punishment for a third offence and yet I still didn't get my act together."

"That's me to a tee," I concurred. "I can never get myself organised, but then I've never been threatened with the cane."

"Mmmmmm."

She looked at me quizzically and then carried on with her story.

"When my tutor discovered I'd failed to hand it in on time yet again, he just said I would attend the Headmistress's 10 o'clock session the following morning. My knees buckled a little when I heard him say this and, at the same time, several of my fellow students sniggered. Having those other young men and women laughing with delight at my predicament was the first stage of a punishment which was cleverly designed to build through a number of different stages between then and half past ten the following morning, when I walked out of the Headmistress's study clutching my burning bum, desperately trying to rub out the throbbing pain."

"The first and last stages?" I enquired, fascinated.

"Yes. Actually, come to think of it, that wasn't the last stage of the punishment. I suppose that was when I returned to my class with a few tears still in my eyes and gingerly eased myself to sit down on the hard wooden chair which was mine. I remember perching on the edge of the seat, holding my sore buttocks in the air just above the unforgiving wooden surface. Even this was difficult to do as the Headmistress had caned the tops of my thighs as well as my buttocks, so that made sitting on the edge a very sore, painful business also. There was no way to win with a bottom as sore as mine was."

I was absolutely mesmerised by this vivid description and I don't think I've ever been so turned on.

My cock was rock hard - and throbbing as much as my attractive new friend's 18-year-old bum had been on that painful Friday morning. I had to find out more.

"You said the laughter in class was just the first stage of the punishment," I ventured. "And going back to class and trying to sit down was the last, so what happened in between?"

"Well," Olivia replied, clearly warming to her subject. "Stage two was the waiting. The Headmistress always did her caning on a Friday morning. This was when she punished all the pupils who'd deserved it during the week. Being told my fate on the Thursday meant I had to think about my impending appointment with the Headmistress's cane all through the rest of that day and, in particular, during the night."

"You can't have got much sleep?" I suggested.

"Quite," she said. "It's very difficult to sleep when you know you're going to be submissively presenting you bottom for painful punishment in the morning. I already knew that the Headmistress's cane hurt like absolute hell. It stung like a thousand vipers in a narrow line of excruciating burning fire, which increased with every stroke she applied to your exposed arse."

"Wow!" I said, getting turned on even more by the fact that she'd casually spoken of an exposed arse. She was one sexy woman!

"Yes. The thought of that happening to you very soon certainly concentrates your mind!"

"Wow indeed!" was all I could say.

"Stage three was when you presented yourself outside her door at the appointed time. On the occasion I'm describing there were three of us sixth formers nervously standing there, shuffling from foot to foot, staring at the floor silently, thinking about what awaited us inside the study. Two young men waiting to be caned – and me!"

"Wow!" I said, mesmerised.

"On the dot of half past ten, the door would open and we'd be summoned to enter. 'Step inside, ladies and gentlemen, won't you?' she'd say sarcastically, as though she was inviting us in for a social call or a business meeting. Then would follow a long lecture regarding our misdemeanours and the need for us to suffer discipline as a consequence. All the time, the cane would be lying on her desk waiting to carry out its burning, excruciating retribution for our sins."

"I suppose your eyes kept looking at the cane as she spoke," I said.

"Yes, absolutely. You were just drawn to it in a strange sort of way. Once the lecture was over, she'd announce the name of the first student who was to be punished."

"Could be in any order, I suppose?" I asked.

"Yes, which only increased the tension. We all knew the score. You had to hang your blazer on the back of the door, and then walk over to the big leather-topped desk. You had to drop your skirt or trousers, step out of them and hang them up as well. These were followed by your panties which, again, you had to hang on the hook with your other clothes. All this while your mates were watching in complete silence and stomach-churning apprehension. Finally, you had to bend over to present your bare bottom, not only for the caning but also for your mates and the Headmistress to view."

"Couldn't you just quickly drop your skirt and panties?" I enquired innocently.

"You couldn't just drop your skirt and panties to your ankles. You had to take them right off because your legs had to be spread as wide apart as they would go."

"Spread wide apart?" I was incredulous. I couldn't believe what I was hearing.

"Yes. You also had to grip the far side of the table and then go up on tiptoe to push your bottom right up and out for the cane. With your legs spread wide, your bum cheeks were spread wide also –

exposing your most private place of all and, at the same time, enabling the cane to find the softer inner parts of each of your cheeks every time it struck. The Headmistress would often spend quite a while adjusting your position so that your bottom was exactly as she wanted it, for the punishment to be as effective as possible."

"But that must have been incredibly embarrassing," I said as my manhood grew bigger and strained against the inside of my pants.

"Absolutely. It was extremely embarrassing, with several of your mates watching. Once in position, it was absolutely forbidden for you to move. If you did, you always got extra strokes or sometimes, if you were getting, say, 12 strokes and you moved on stroke number seven, she'd go right back to the beginning and start again from number one. Now that DOES hurt, because your buttocks are sore and much more sensitive by then."

"Sounds like your Headmistress was a very proficient caner," I said.

"Yes. She was a real expert with the cane, as you can tell, and took great pride in the discipline she gave. She knew the cane always improved behaviour no end."

This idea really resonated with me. The idea of behaviour being changed by a painful caning was completely new to me. At my school, we'd been able to behave any way we liked without the fear of any consequence. Numerous pupils were regularly late, dozens of us openly swore at our teachers, and more or less everyone had a couldn't-care-less attitude to our work that went completely unchecked. No one ever criticised us. All the teachers just praised us, no matter what rubbish we handed in. Some of them even THANKED us for doing our essays or whatever! Can you imagine that?

"Yes, as I say," Olivia was continuing, "the cane always changes the recipient's behaviour and improves it no end. It hurts so much, you see, that you don't want to repeat the experience if you can help it. My behaviour certainly improved radically after the particular caning I'm telling you about."

"Did you ever see your Headmistress again after you left school?" I asked.

"Yes. I met our old Headmistress at a school reunion several years later and she told me that she always got great pleasure out of using the cane, particularly on sixth-formers. She liked the feeling of authority and power it gave her, she liked seeing the way young men and women were visibly frightened by just the threat of it, and she gained great satisfaction from seeing the tremendous improvements in behaviour that every application of the cane always achieved."

"Wow!"

"I think, on a practical level, our wonderful Headmistress also took great satisfaction from creating nice neat sets of tramlines all the way down our bums, that were horizontal and evenly spaced on both buttocks."

"So, corporal punishment was frequent in your school?" I asked, pleased with myself for knowing the correct terminology.

"Yes. She used her favourite cane regularly and enthusiastically, with never a Friday going by without at least one young man presenting himself for its painful benefits. It was rarer for the young women, certainly, and rare for us to receive six of the best."

"What, just a couple of strokes was the norm?"

"No! She never thought even six was enough, always preferring twelve strokes to really drive the message home and ensure the lesson was learnt.

On occasions, it would be eighteen but this was always the maximum. If she thought more than this was warranted, you would return the following Friday to complete your allocation."

"Return for more?" I was astounded.

"Yes. I remember a particularly lazy, rude, insolent young man who really tried the tutor's patience time and again. Eventually he was awarded 36 strokes, all to be applied HARD to his bare bottom, with 18 strokes the first Friday and another 18 the next week. His bum was still striped and sore when he went back after seven days, but that didn't deter the Headmistress from carrying out the rest of the well-deserved punishment as hard as she could. She was a very firm believer in the benefits of corporal punishment – as I am myself."

I was shaking a little as I heard all this. That last remark was certainly said to cause me concern.

Olivia owned a real school cane. I'd seen it in the hall, and the way the conversation was going made me begin to wonder whether I'd be discovering its effects for myself before the evening was out.

"And the most important stage?" I enquired innocently.

"The caning itself, obviously," Olivia snapped.

"As I've said, the Headmistress was a real expert in corporal punishment, and an absolute enthusiast. She was able to give a caning which was a skilful combination of the dialogue and the pain. The dialogue was designed to embarrass you and cause panic, and the actual strokes of the cane were designed to hurt as much as possible without doing you any real, lasting harm. A lethal but extremely effective regime!"

I wanted to know more about the dialogue. I was starting to appreciate that the dialogue might turn me on. I couldn't imagine how the phenomenally painful strokes could make me horny, but I could see that the dialogue might.

"What did she say to you exactly?" I enquired innocently.

"Let's have that bottom right up for its punishment, young lady!"

"That's pretty humiliating," I stated.

"Yes, or sometimes she'd say things like …. We'll see if another twelve strokes will produce the desired effect. If not, you can return next Friday for a further dozen."

"That would concentrate your mind!" I said with not a little enthusiasm. Was I starting to get keen on the whole thing? But then, what about the pain involved? There would be a huge amount of that!

"I can remember more or less exactly what she said one time," Olivia told me.

"It was to do with the business I've just discussed — where you'd have to come back again the next week for more. She said, most young men and women who visit me twice for two of my canings quickly realise the error of their ways. I like to make sure that my canings always bring about complete regret in the recipient!"

"Wow!"

"Or sometimes she'd say things like ....

I'm sure you've remembered from previous visits to my study that I always make the last couple of strokes the hardest, and you'll discover, if you don't know already, that I always apply them across the lowest part of your bottom, right where you sit down.

or .... I shan't remind you again that you need to keep still. If there is any more wriggling or writhing of your buttocks, I shall cane the tops of your legs HARD and then continue caning your bottom."

All these examples were more than enough for me. By now, my throbbing member was rock hard and desperate for relief.

Mrs Hamilton was having an almost hypnotic effect on me. I was truly afraid of her cane and what she clearly could do with it, yet I was mesmerised by her enthusiasm, experience and obvious skill.

Something within me wanted to try it out for myself – but I was understandably terrified. She had me hooked, well and truly, and I think, by the look on her face, she knew it.

Eventually things took a new turn. Olivia stopped talking, sat back and looked me straight in the eyes.

"You're interested in all this, aren't you!" she announced, quite confidently.

CHAPTER THREE – ADMITTING I NEED PUNISHMENT

I looked down at the floor and gulped. Finally, I spoke too.

"Yes Miss, I think I am. You see, no one has ever disciplined me. All through my life so far, I've been able to do more or less as I please. I've known inside that a lot of what I've done has been wrong, but no one has ever corrected me. You're the first person who's ever suggested such a thing. It's compelling, but it's terrifying at the same time. I'm starting to feel that I want to submit to you, but obviously, I'm afraid of how much it will hurt."

"It NEEDS to hurt," Olivia explained. "That's how my cane will free you from the guilt you feel. It will sting like the very devil, but it will cleanse you of all your past mistakes. And besides, I would never dream of doing anything to you that would really harm you."

"But it will hurt like blazes, surely?"

"Yes, you can be absolutely sure of that. No one ever imagines just how much a school cane hurts. You won't believe it until you experience it. Then you will NEVER forget. It's just an indescribable pain that burns and stings and penetrates like a thousand vipers – all in one narrow line of fire."

"Wow!"

"But my cane will only do you good. No heavy beating. No lasting damage or injuries. Just a burning, scalding bottom, proudly displaying bright red stripes that throb for a day or two. And a reminder every time you sit down that you've been disciplined – caned hard for your own good. Now how does that sound?"

It didn't take me a moment to say "It sounds good, Miss. Very good. I can see you can really help me."

"Yes, you're right. I can," Olivia smiled. "You're not a bad young man. Just the product of this society's stupid, idiotic child-centred education system. May I suggest that you think about what I've said, and then come back to see me for what we'll call a practical demonstration of my discipline techniques."

And so it was that the mould was set.

On my way home I realised that I hadn't actually asked to see the cane that was so prominently displayed in the hall stand. If I could have held it, felt it, run my fingers along its shiny length, I might have consoled myself that it would probably be quite mild.

But then again, I might have seen just how capable it was of inflicting real pain.

Maybe it was for the best that I just didn't know. The first time I would find out exactly what it could do would be when it landed across my meekly presented bottom – if I decided to go through with what Olivia was suggesting.

That petrified me – and turned me on more and more as I thought about it.

Apart from the actual discipline and the humiliation which would be a necessary part of it, the fact that it was consensual made it all the hornier for some strange reason. I would have to agree to her spanking and caning me. I would have to actually ask her to do it. I would be voluntarily baring my bottom for her to punish, and she would only do it if I actually asked her to.

How humiliating was that?

At work the next day I found it harder than usual to concentrate. My colleague Laura seemed unduly chirpy when it came to coffee break time and I made the mistake of asking her why.

"I'm enjoying the fact that you've been to see my aunt," she chuckled. "I know what she'll have suggested and I'm fascinated to know if you're going to agree."

I stopped dead in my tracks. Laura was looking me right in the eyes as she laughed out loud.

"I'm aware of my aunt's little hobby. She's very good at it. I know that for a fact – but she's never tried it out on me!"

It was quite a while before I was able to speak. Eventually I blurted out

"Are you talking about her discipline?"

"Yes, if that's what she calls spanking and caning the bare arses of good-looking young men for their benefit and her pleasure."

I blushed bright red.

Then she added "You won't be the first, and you won't be the last. You'll just be the next in a long line of young men who've writhed and yelped under the relentless sting of her thin, flexible cane.

They tell me it smarts, burns and stings like blazes!"

This was the very expression I'd used myself when discussing it with Mrs Hamilton.

She chuckled again. "So, have you agreed to submit?" she enquired.

"No I bloody haven't!" I retorted.

"But you're thinking about it, aren't you?" she laughed. "Go on, admit it. You get horny thinking about it, don't you? But that's because you don't know yet just how much it hurts."

"I'm thinking it will do me good," I admitted reluctantly. "She says that hard discipline will do me good. I've never had any discipline in my life. I've never had anyone care about me enough to offer it, and I want to find out what it's like."

"Oh, you'll find out all right!" Laura spluttered.

"Do you know exactly what she does?" I asked tentatively.

"Yes, I do," Laura replied. "I've witnessed lots of her discipline sessions so I've got a pretty good idea of what you've got in store if you consent to her dealing with you. And that's the 64 000-dollar question. Are you going to bend over for her? Before you answer that, let me tell you that even just the bending over is not as simple as it might seem."

"What do you mean?"

"Well," Laura replied brightly, "I've never seen a guy caned across his trousers, or even his pants. She always administers all her discipline on bare buttocks - YOUR bare buttocks in your case – and she takes ages getting you to present your bottom correctly for her. You can expect to have to stick it up at just the right angle for her cane to have the maximum effect, and you'll have to part your legs as wide as they can possibly go. Just think what that shows her."

I gulped and blushed even redder as she continued.

"Have you ever had to display your arsehole to an older woman? Not just to expose it for its own sake, but put it on display for her to punish. Just think about that."

I DID think about that. I thought a lot about it before I managed to stammer my next question.

"Does she cane hard?" I asked.

"Are you joking? Of course she ALWAYS canes hard," was Laura's immediate reply with an assured laugh.

"My aunt doesn't believe in doing anything by half measures so you can be assured that every stroke will be an absolute winner. There's no point otherwise, is there?"

I gulped.

I considered her choice of the word "winner". Did that mean that I would be the loser?

"She thinks that a caning should always result in a change of behaviour which can only be brought about by producing an extremely sore butt. I've heard her say so many times. She makes sure that her canings hurt as much as possible and she always increases the severity of the strokes as she goes along – the last stroke of all being the hardest."

"I don't think I can do this," I said, hearing this.

"No. Don't get me wrong. It's not heavy beating or anything. There's no need for that, she'll say. She won't do you any lasting harm but you'll find the pain absolutely intolerable from the very first stroke and you'll find it almost impossible to keep meekly presenting your bottom for more."

"Wow!"

"I've spoken to guys who've gone to her quite confidently, thinking it'll be a breeze. Her favourite cane very quickly reduces guys like that to begging and pleading, gasping and yelping uncontrollably. Brings them down a peg or two which is only a good thing. And then there's the after effects."

"After effects?" I stuttered.

"Yes. Don't expect to be able to sit down comfortably for the rest of the day. Guys tell me they have to perch on the edge of the chair to avoid putting their throbbing, burning buttocks in contact with a hard seat. They say it feels like they've sat on an electric fire. Your arse will feel like it's literally been scalded by all those severe stinging strokes."

I was enormously embarrassed by now. The fact that Laura knew all about her aunt's methods in such detail, and the fact that she knew I was likely to be finding out for myself the effects her aunt could achieve with her cane – all this couldn't have been more humiliating for me. And Laura understood this only too well.

"Having second thoughts?" she asked. "Going to chicken out, or are you up for the challenge? You'll feel great if you can get through it. Everybody does. But it's not easy. My aunt makes sure of that."

"I'm not chickening out," I stated categorically.

"Well, in that case, why don't you ask me a few more questions? Just to set your mind at rest – or NOT, as the case may be!"

"OK," I said. "How many strokes will I get?"

"She always canes in sixes," Laura told me. "The traditional six of the best. So you'll probably get three sixes. That's her usual allocation. Don't worry. She'll take her time. You'll probably get corner time in between each six, and if you're good, and totally obedient, you won't get any extra treatments."

"Extra treatments?"

"Yes. Like standing in the corner, say. She'll always give very clear instructions but that's the point. You'll have to adhere to them. It's all part of learning true discipline. It's very good for you in the long run. You'll be told to stand in the corner, hands on your head and no rubbing."

"No rubbing?"

"Yes. With your bum on fire and stinging like blazes, the natural thing to do is to rub your buttocks to try to rub out the pain. That's forbidden by my aunt. If you do, you'll get your hands caned. She'll tell you hands are for placing on your head, not for rubbing your scalded bottom – and then she'll give you a hand-caning to remind you."

I didn't want my hands caned. I was sure of that. I just couldn't imagine how much THAT would hurt.

"Which hand would she cane?" I asked, really embarrassed now.

"It doesn't matter which hand you hold out for her first, because she always canes both of them," Laura told me confidently.

"Both of them?"

Again, I was incredulous.

Laura nonchalantly took another sip of her coffee.

"She canes alternate hands. The first stroke on your right, let's say, and then the second stroke on your left. That's the relatively easy bit, although the cane does have a particularly painful bite when used across the palms, guys tell me. The hardest bit is holding your right hand out again for a second stroke when it's already stinging so much. It's a penetrating sort of sting, apparently, which seems to go deep into your palm, and of course it increases as more strokes are applied."

"MORE strokes? How many strokes do you get on your hands?"

"She always canes alternate hands as I say, and she always canes in sixes, so the very minimum hand caning she gives is three on each. Quite a challenge to take for any man at any age, and then of course you go back into the corner for the originally allotted time plus an extra fifteen minutes, with your hands burning on the top of your head and your bottom burning behind you."

"That's mind-blowing," I said.

"Yes. All the time, you know you're going to be meekly bending back over again soon for the next six strokes across your arse. And remember the strokes get harder all the time as she goes along. Do you see what my aunt means by discipline? And do you see the good it would do you to live under that sort of regime? She'll make a man out of you for the first time and you'll start to feel much better about yourself."

I was totally overwhelmed by now. My mind was racing and I felt quite numb. Deep down inside, I knew the answer. I knew what I had to do.

I had to call Olivia and ask her to take me on. I had to ask her to change my life.

It was a long time before I said to Laura, with complete humility, "You're right. I do see what you mean and I do understand the good your aunt can do me."

Laura beamed. "Good man!" she said. "I'm proud of you already, and don't worry. She'll never do you any harm and you'll start to reap the benefits from your first visit."

It was at that very moment that coffee time ended and we returned to our positions behind the counter. A customer was waiting and I said

"Let me deal with this one, Laura ...... Good morning Miss. May I help you?"

Olivia's cane – or just the thought of it – was already having a beneficial and positive effect on my behaviour.

My mind was soon made up, and so ...

It was the following Tuesday when I finally made the phone call. The day had dawned brightly, with warm sunshine streaming in through my window.

Birds twittered in the tall oak tree at the end of the garden as I opened the curtains and threw open the window. It seemed the kind of day to get things done, to get something underway that had been playing on my mind for quite some time.

I'd had several days of mental torment and restless, sleepless nights. It was the nights that had been the hardest. Well, to put it another way, it was DURING the nights that my cock had been the hardest.

I was in complete turmoil. How could I agree to what Olivia was proposing? But, on the other hand, how could I turn down this incredible, unique opportunity?

I knew the discipline would undoubtedly benefit me – and I also knew that it was going to turn me on like nothing ever had before.

Then again, I knew it was going to be very embarrassing and extremely painful. More painful than I could ever have imagined, as it turned out! Just as she had said it would be.

I waited until just after 9 am before I found myself dialling Mrs Hamilton's number.

"Olivia Hamilton!"

"Um, yes, it's Daniel ... Miss!"

"Ah, yes. I've been waiting to hear from you. I'd almost given you up."

"Sorry Miss. I've found it really difficult to know what I want."

"I know what you want, and that's good, HARD discipline. Now it seems YOU finally know what you want as well ... so I'm very pleased to hear it."

"Yes Miss. I DO know what I want now, Miss. I want you to discipline me ... please Miss."

"Excellent!" Olivia sounded triumphant. "And when is the earliest time you can report to me?"

"After work this evening Miss."

"We'll say six o'clock then. Shower very thoroughly, put on clean underpants, dress smartly overall, and report promptly at six."

"Yes Miss."

"And what kind of pants do you wear?"

This was the first inkling of the humiliation Olivia was going to be putting me through.

"Um, boxer briefs, Miss."

"Good man. They'll be coming down when I'm ready, but you'll look fine in those during your initial corner time. Six o'clock. Don't be late or there'll be another penalty to pay. Do you get the idea? That's what discipline is all about!"

There was a sharp click followed by an incessant burrrrr indicating that she'd put the phone down. My appointment had been made and there was no going back. This was it. I was going to be disciplined for the first time in my life, and it was going to HURT.

CHAPTER FOUR - MY FIRST PAINFUL EXPERIENCE OF THE CANE

I realised I was actually shaking as I carefully opened Olivia's front gate.

Everything about her house was ordered and tidy and the same applied to her garden – even the gate. It was made of beautifully painted wood. A dark green surround with cream painted vertical slats in the middle.

I walked up the path between the two immaculately maintained lawns that looked virtually manicured in their preciseness.

It wasn't a stark garden. It had lots of colour. Bright reds, yellows and oranges shone from the abundant beds which were filled with glorious plants and flowers of all kinds. It felt like a happy garden. The garden of someone with a positive outlook on life.

Tentatively I knocked on the big front door with the brass door knocker provided for the purpose. My knock was so light that I immediately wondered if she would hear. I was too nervous, however, to knock again.

After what seemed an eternity I heard footsteps coming along the hallway.

The door opened.

"Ah! My new young charge. Right on time too!" Olivia sounded confident and pleased. "Come in, won't you?"

She was so polite and welcoming – warm even, that I started to feel a little better myself as I stepped inside.

While she was closing the door, my eyes fell on the umbrella stand at the far end where, on my previous visit, I had seen the thin school cane waiting in readiness to be put to use. It was no longer there.

As soon as the door was shut her manner changed.

"You know why you're here, so let's not waste any time in getting started. Take off all your clothes except your pants and then come into the study."

I froze with embarrassment. "What, here Miss?" I asked.

"Yes of course here," she snapped. "And if there's one thing I don't like it's having my instructions questioned. Another time that would have earned you an extra six strokes, but as this is your first visit for discipline I will overlook it just this once. Take off all your clothes except your underpants. You can place them all on that small table over there and then, when you're ready, you can come in to see me. I will then explain the various stages of your discipline and the individual punishments involved."

She turned and walked away down the corridor, through the open doorway that I knew led to her study. I started to undress. Feeling as nervous as I did, everything took longer than it might have done.

My shirt and vest were off, along with my shoes and socks. I was just hopping on one foot with my trousers around one ankle when there was a knock at the door. It was a confident knock, far louder than mine had been.

I froze in horror. I was nearly naked. My trousers were down and the only covering for my modesty was my pants which provided very little protection, being very thin white cotton briefs.

Olivia Hamilton was striding along the hall, and as she passed me she said "Oh! Did I tell you Jennifer is joining us?"

I was completely unable to reply. My trousers finally came off and I was left standing in my boxer briefs with my hands clasped in front of them as the door flew open. Bright sunshine streamed in as I saw a smartly dressed, very upright elderly woman standing there.

"Jennifer! Good to see you," Olivia was saying. "Come along in. Our young friend is just getting ready as you can see!"

The two friends paid no attention to me as they walked together through to the study. I stood for a moment, confused, concerned. Then I realised I'd been told to go into the study as soon as I had stripped to my pants.

Reluctantly I walked along the corridor and into the room where I found the two of them seated relaxedly sipping white wine. I had never felt so vulnerable and exposed.

My hands were still clasped tightly in front of my pants in a futile attempt to cover the bulge in them which was involuntarily increasing in size as I took in my situation.

"There's no need for modesty," Olivia announced. "You haven't got anything that Dr Hargreaves and I have not seen many times, I can assure you. This is Jennifer who is a very good friend of mine. DOCTOR Jennifer Hargreaves. Like me she's a great believer in the efficacy of corporal punishment and she often enjoys spectating my discipline sessions."

"Good evening, young man," Dr Hargreaves said politely.

"Good evening, Dr Hargreaves," was all I could say in reply.

"The lovely Dr Hargreaves has kindly agreed to spectate your disciplinary session this evening and I know she'll give us some very good feedback as she watches your reaction. She's not only an enthusiast but a bit of a novice practitioner herself so she may well have ideas that will enhance your punishments here this evening."

"Enhanced punishments?"

"Please don't question my terminology. You've made a number of mistakes, as we discussed when you were last here, and I know you're already sorry for them. Between us, Dr Hargreaves and I will make sure your regret is complete."

I blushed bright red as I took all this in. I remembered how Olivia had told me the previous week how she always made sure her canings brought about complete regret. Now she was going to give me a practical demonstration of how she achieved that!

"Take down your pants, place them over the back of the armchair, and then go over to the corner by the bookcase. Stand with your nose right against the wall and your hands on your head. You are not to move until I tell you to. In the meantime, you can contemplate what you discipline is likely to consist of."

"Yes Miss," was all I could say.

I pulled my pants down over my tumescent manhood, exposing my creamy smooth, slightly hairy cheeks which were for the moment completely unblemished. How long would they remain that way? I walked over to the corner, placed my nose against the wall, my feet well apart and my hands on my head.

My discipline had begun.

The longer I waited, the more anxious I became.

I'd seen the cane and asked about it, but I still wasn't sure whether it was going to be used on me. It was surely only used as the ultimate sanction, I kept telling myself, and I hadn't been as bad as all that.

Strangely, along with the anxiety, I was becoming more and more aroused.

My semi-tumescent member seemed to have a mind of its own as I stood to attention, naked in front of these two older people. I knew I mustn't touch it. I couldn't touch it in any case, as my hands were on my head, but the more I thought about what Olivia might be going to do to me, the more stiff it became. When I started to think about submitting to her in front of the beautiful and voluptuous Dr Hargreaves, it stuck straight up, proud and hard, throbbing.

I didn't know at that point that it would be a VERY long time before I would be able to get any relief.

Cum control over long periods would turn out to be a significant part of Olivia Hamilton's discipline regime. I'll tell you all about it later. For the moment, I just stood there very embarrassed and increasingly anxious minute by minute.

The two friends relaxed as they chatted about the best treatment for me to receive and reminisced about times past.

"I'll tell you what Olivia, If I'd been as rude and thoughtless as this young man has been .... well, in my day, I'd have been unable to sit down for a week," Dr Hargreaves said, matter-of-factly.

Mrs Hamilton leaned back in her armchair and looked quite pleased as her friend made this remark.

"Indeed," she replied. "The young men of today have no idea of discipline. They don't understand the good time-honoured methods of days gone by. They have no experience of the effects of a good caning – or the benefits. We need to punish him properly while he's here with us this evening. We need to drive the lesson home so that he doesn't do it again."

I started to shake a little.

"Absolutely," Dr Hargreaves agreed. "Before you begin, though, it would surely be a good idea to go through all his misdemeanours and then devise an appropriate punishment for each. A complete discipline regime will benefit him enormously."

"Yes, quite," Olivia concurred. "It will really pay him dividends."

"Do you intend applying all the discipline to his bottom?" Dr Hargreaves pondered, looking quizzically at her extremely sexy friend.

My cock twitched.

"The majority can be given that way ... but there are still plenty of other sanctions that can be very effective."

All I could do was listen in silence and wait.

"Such as?" Jennifer enquired.

"Line writing, hand caning – and of course smacking the backs of his legs. The cane can be very successfully applied to the legs and thighs too."

Mrs Hamilton was very matter of fact about these unbelievably painful and humiliating suggestions – especially the last one, I thought.

I didn't exactly know what a leg smacking would feel like, but I felt absolutely sure it would be something I would find extremely unpleasant and embarrassing.

"The cane can be effectively applied to hands or bottom – or both," Dr Hargreaves added brightly, with quite an enthusiastic glint in her eye.

"I agree," Olivia replied. "I always concentrate on a young man's bottom when I give one of my hard, prolonged canings, but, then again, a hand caning is an ideal additional punishment if there's been any disobedience or resistance during the caning of the arse!"

Olivia Hamilton coming out with the word "arse" somewhat surprised me. She was so formal, so contained and collected, that I wouldn't have imagined her using such a word so casually, now that my discipline had begun.

I remembered her using such a term when she'd been describing her punishments as a sixth former, but that didn't seem so inappropriate then, somehow. The fact that she did so now, knowing I was listening, and knowing that it was my arse they were discussing, turned me on even more.

My cock twitched more urgently and started to drip a little pre-cum. I desperately wanted to rub it – but I couldn't, in front of these two female friends.

"Surely, it's time for Daniel to list his mistakes," Jennifer suggested. "What are we waiting for?"

"Absolutely!" Olivia agreed. She turned to face me.

"Come over here, still keeping your hands on your head. Stand in front of me and tell me why you need to be disciplined and punished. List your wrongdoings loudly and clearly please so that we can all hear. When you have done so, young man, Jennifer and I will agree on the best method of dealing with them," Olivia said with some satisfaction.

I looked at them with even more anxiety, but couldn't bring myself to say anything. I walked slowly over to the attractive woman who was now going to be my Mistress.

With my hands on my head, my stiff manhood stood out proudly in front of me. When I arrived in front of Olivia who was sitting on quite a low armchair, it was more or less level with her face. This was something new to me. I'd never been in such a position before. I still remained silent, embarrassed, nervous, humiliated.

"Speak up, man!" Jennifer commanded. "We haven't got all day."

I stuttered and stammered a bit – and then managed to say...

"I suppose my biggest mistakes are rudeness and laziness, Dr Hargreaves. I was rude to Olivia in the shop – and I'm frequently rude to loads of people. I used to be extremely rude to my teachers when I was in the sixth form, but, looking back, I'd say a lot of it was their fault as they never used to even TRY to correct us."

"This is not the time to discuss the stupidity of the modern education system," Olivia said sharply. "You admit that your first mistake is rudeness and it will certainly be dealt with in a manner you won't forget."

"Yes Miss."

Jennifer took a sip from her cup of tea as she said...

"Everyone knows a good, thorough caning is the most painful and effective discipline for a grown man or woman to experience. I can certainly vouch for that myself, having been on the receiving end too many times to remember in my youthful days! And of course, it isn't going to be any the less painful whatever age you are."

She unthinkingly rubbed her full and shapely arse through her expensive trousers as she said this. Although she was now elderly, she was still a sexy woman.

"The cane is the perfect remedy for rudeness. Do you agree Olivia?"

Olivia Hamilton sat up straight and said "I certainly do! It's my favourite instrument to use for numerous reasons. The school cane is always the most feared of all corporal punishment implements and indeed, I always aim to make sure my pupil does truly fear my cane. Just the sight of it can cause alarm and panic for many of my recalcitrant pupils."

Even Jennifer looked a little uncomfortable as Olivia looked straight at her and continued.

"You're obviously someone who knows from plenty of experience the effects it can produce, Jennifer. I always cane hard – to get the results I want to see. I always achieve visual results – nice, long, clear red lines painted horizontally across both cheeks – and vocal results, which can include begging, pleading, yelping, gasping – and even shouting."

Jennifer chuckled. "Good!" she said. "Sounds like you're a real expert. I shall enjoy a nice, loud vocal reaction – if we get one from Daniel."

"Oh, we WILL," Olivia concurred. "I shall make damn sure of that – from the very first stroke."

These remarks had an instant effect on me. My throbbing manhood stopped straining upwards and started to descend. My knees buckled and it was all I could do to remain standing.

"The sight of the cane can cause alarm and panic," Olivia had just said.

Well, the cane had been in my sight throughout their conversation. Olivia had positioned me so that I was facing the far corner where it stood leaning against the wall.

The two friends had both agreed that the cane had benefited them when they were growing up. I had never had the cane and now I was going to "benefit" from its effects too.

I started to shuffle from foot to foot ... until Olivia said "Stand still, can't you? If you shuffle around any more, I'll add your fidgeting to the list of transgressions that I'm going to deal with."

"Yes Miss," was all I could say.

"What kind of canes do you use?" Jennifer asked. "Do you have more than one?"

"Yes, I have several." Olivia replied. "That's my favourite over there in the corner. It's my favourite because of its flexibility, its diameter and its crooked handle. A punishment cane needs to be flexible rattan or kooboo, preferably with a curved handle which not only adds to the traditional appearance but also enables it to be hung up permanently in view, to serve as a constant reminder of what awaits a transgressor."

"Not bamboo garden cane, then?"

"Bamboo garden cane will definitely not do! It is stiff and completely unsuitable. I have several high-quality canes of varying thicknesses, all of which are very flexible and whippy, and hurt like absolute blazes from the very first stroke."

"You clearly know a lot about the subject" Jennifer said, with some obvious admiration. "Before you begin your demonstration on young Daniel's arse right here, tell us ... why does a caning hurt so much? I'm sure Daniel would be fascinated to know."

She said this with quite a smirk and reached over to help herself to another biscuit as I listened to Olivia Hamilton's typically long-winded explanation.

I started to see that all this dialogue was deliberate. It was designed to produce panic and real distress for me as the waiting miscreant – and it was certainly succeeding!

"The flexibility of a discipline cane is what makes it so painful," Olivia said, going over to the corner and picking up what she'd said to be her favourite cane. She stroked its slender length, rubbed its crook handle and tip, then bent it into a perfect arc.

"It whips and stings like nothing else, producing a fine line of fire across properly presented bottom cheeks. Humiliating and painful in the olden days for a sixth former who had to report for punishment. Scorching, burning and deeply penetrating pain from each stroke builds up throughout the traditional six or twelve of the best so that the recipient can be quickly reduced to uncontrolled gasping and yelping, begging for the punishment to stop. That's certainly the effect I aim to achieve this evening. And I always do! Come over here Daniel!"

I was shaking much more as I walked over to Mrs Hamilton, my hands still upon my head. She spoke quite kindly to me as she took hold of both my hands and gently glided them down to my sides. Was it just by accident that her hands brushed against my cock as she continued to speak?

"We're just about at the point of no return, Daniel." she said. "Please remember that what I'm going to do to you is for your own good. More to the point, it's consensual. After all you've heard, are you sure you want to go ahead? You're free to go if you'd rather. You can put your clothes on, walk out of my house and nothing more will ever be said. My cane will remain over there in the corner and your bottom will not suffer at all. Tell me honestly what you think, Daniel."

She smiled and very, very lightly brushed her hands across my chest, tweaking my nipples momentarily. Her hands descended to gently cup my full balls as she waited for my reply.

"I want to stay, Miss." I whispered.

Her hands gripped my balls more tightly.

"It will be very, very painful for you," she reminded me. "Humiliating too. That's an essential part of the discipline that always makes it so effective."

"I know Miss. I want to submit to you completely. I've made a real mess of my life so far and you're the first person who's offered to sort me out."

Olivia let go of me and stood up straight. "You're learning already," she said warmly. "You're beginning to turn into quite a wise young man."

"Thank you, Miss," I replied.

"Now, one final time" Olivia spoke with real authority. "You can leave or you can stay. The decision is only yours, not mine. If you decide to stay, I hope you can see that you can trust me completely. I will never do you any harm. Only good."

"Yes Miss."

"My whippy cane will take you to the very edge of the pain that you think you can stand ... and then I'll take you even further. You'll squeal, you'll writhe, you'll wriggle and you'll beg me to stop – but I won't, young man, until you've REALLY learned your lessons. And you've got quite a few to learn. We'll take them one by one and we'll deal with each one thoroughly and completely."

"Yes Miss. Er ... yes please Miss."

"You've admitted to rudeness and laziness, which I imagine is manifested in a general lack of application to tasks you're given to do."

"Yes Miss."

"And what else have you done that you regret?"

This was the moment of no return. This was the moment when I managed to tell them about the terrible way I'd treated my wife.

I stuttered and stammered, but I managed to give them a clear impression of what I'd done. I told them everything, including the divorce. In a strange way, I almost started to feel better just by telling them. I began to see that I might feel better still if I were punished for this.

The two friends listened carefully and seriously. Then Olivia said

"I think you can probably see that I'm someone who can realistically deal with all the mistakes you've told us about. You know my methods now, so ... what do you say?"

There was a long silence as I considered what she had said. She and Jennifer looked straight at me as they waited for my response. A caning couldn't really be too bad, could it, I told myself. And if I left now I'd never know what it felt like.

Also, I liked Olivia a lot. She was clearly a fine woman of high principles and not the kind of person I'd come across before. She wouldn't REALLY hurt me. Or would she? I would shortly find out!

Finally, I spoke up.

"I say ... Yes please Miss. Please discipline me. Please cane me."

Mrs Hamilton came right up close to me and whispered in my ear.

"How?" she enquired. "HOW shall I cane you?"

I gulped and paused before I added ... "Please cane me HARD Miss."

Mrs Hamilton gave a satisfied grin as she spoke – loudly this time, and with real authority.

"Oh, I will, young man. I will! Don't you worry about that!"

Olivia Hamilton smiled broadly and Jennifer sat back in her armchair looking very contentedly settled.

CHAPTER FIVE - MORE IMAGINATIVE PUNISHMENTS

"I think we will begin," Olivia announced. "Go over to the chaise longue and kneel on it facing the wall. Put your head right down with your elbows out. Now stick your bottom up as far as it will go and spread your legs wide open."

I was almost more confident now as I walked over to comply with my instructions.

I knelt up, put my head down onto the soft surface of the bed and turned it to the right resting on my hands. My forearms rested on the bed also, with my elbows out to the left and right.

This position had the effect of sticking my bum quite lewdly up in the air. I'd been told to part my legs as far as they would go, and when I did this I realised I was opening up my arse to the view of these other two adults.

I felt the cool air in my crack as my cheeks parted, revealing my most private part and exposing it to my adult spectators. Two very attractive women could now see every part of me.

Now I knew for the first time what it meant to "present" my bottom for punishment.

I waited, breathing heavily, heart beating fast. What had I let myself in for? I would soon find out!

"Quite well presented," Olivia said encouragingly. "But I think we can have your bottom a little higher still for its punishment. Stick it right up lad!"

She spoke sharply and I obeyed immediately. Now I couldn't be more submissive.

"I guess he's going to really feel these strokes!" Jennifer said, pouring herself another glass of wine and moving forward onto the edge of her chair. "This is a really smooth pinot grigio, nicely chilled." She took a gentle sip and relaxed.

"Have you got a good view of the proceedings there, Jennifer?" Olivia asked.

"Oh yes, excellent!" Jennifer replied. "How many is he getting?"

"Either six or twelve – depending," Olivia said.

"Depending on how he takes them?" Jennifer enquired. "Do you adjust, or ease off, or whatever, depending on how he copes with the pain?"

All this time, my arse was in the air, meekly waiting for its fate.

"Oh no!" Olivia countered. "I don't alter what I give depending on his reaction. In a realistic hard caning like I give, the guy's vocal and physical response has no bearing on what is being given. In adult discipline, Jennifer, the Mistress merely continues with what has been prescribed, pleased with the effect it is having on the guy who's been misbehaving. And there's no need for anything heavy anyway."

"Of course not," Jennifer concurred.

"Accurate strokes, delivered with just a flick of the wrist will produce an absolutely intolerable sting without doing any real damage. A few harder strokes introduced without warning will literally keep the 'sub' on his toes, and of course the last stroke of any six or twelve should always be the hardest and most memorable."

"But you said 'depending', so what does the number of strokes depend on?"

"It depends on his obedience or, heaven help him, his disobedience," Olivia explained while I continued to stick my bare bottom UP as far as it would go.

"Some guys move out of the position they've been told to adopt for discipline. A slight movement is sometimes inevitable … but anything more than that will always result in my doubling the dose of punishment. Hence my mention of six …. or possibly twelve."

"Yes, I understand," Jennifer said. "And I suppose, whether it's six or twelve strokes he gets, the last stroke will always be the hardest? That's what my Headmistress used to do. We always knew to expect that."

"Yes, exactly," Olivia confirmed. "It's an unspoken rule that both parties – Mistress and pupil - know that this will be the case. It's a nice extra challenge for the 'Top' to be able to give, and it provides an extra incentive for the sub to behave because, throughout the caning, he always knows what to expect for the last stroke."

"Tell Daniel about the last stroke!" Jennifer suggested with a chuckle and a broad grin.

"Well, if he's not able to take any of the regular strokes without a lot of wriggling, writhing and general protest, then he will find the last one absolutely intolerable – and therefore be really dreading it all through the punishment. This will concentrate his mind completely, which is always one of the aims of corporal discipline along with causing increasing pain and humiliation."

At this, Olivia swished her favourite cane through the air several times, producing that classic whooshing sound that always precedes the whack and the thwhipp. I stuck my butt up and braced myself. This was it.

The first thing I felt was not the first stroke.

Olivia was very gently rubbing the cane across my cheeks. It was almost a caress, and it was so gentle that some of the time it wasn't even touching the skin of my buttocks. She managed to rub just the downy hairs which covered my two exposed cheeks. Oh no! I was getting really hard again down there.

Now she was putting the tip of the cane just into my crack, tapping it from side to side, lightly touching the soft inner parts of each of my arse cheeks. Oh, that felt so good.

Then there was a sort of sawing motion as she smoothly ran the length of the cane back and forth across the very crown of my arse, a little above my hole. As I was to discover a moment or two later, this was to mark out the position of the first stroke… where she was going to make it land.

Then it happened. Swish …

THWACK!

With a deft flick of her wrist, Olivia brought the cane down smartly, right across the very middle of my bottom. For a split second, I didn't feel anything. Then ….

"Aaaaaaaargh!" I yelled.

The first stroke of that thin, whippy cane cut right across the centre of my bum. It stung like hell and produced an immediate burning line of fire.

I jumped up, clutching my scalded arse, desperately trying to rub out the searing pain that was completely consuming me.

I danced about the room, my manhood rapidly softening and flopping from side to side as I went. The two female friends said nothing for a minute or two. Then I realised Olivia was still holding the cane, and slowly rubbing its shiny, flexible length.

"I'm waiting," was all she said.

"I can't Miss," I replied. "I'm sorry. I never imagined it would hurt like that. I can't, Miss. I can't take any more."

"You CAN take more, and you WILL." Olivia said extremely firmly. "It's only a few minutes since you agreed that one of my canings was not only what you needed, but was what you actually WANTED. You have had only one stroke, so you have at least another eleven to go. Bend over again and present your bottom correctly for me to continue."

The enormity of this instruction overwhelmed me.

That cane had produced the most excruciating line of burning pain I'd ever experienced. A line of absolute fire that wasn't diminishing at all.

Further strokes would only add to my hurt and distress. I could clearly see that each additional stroke would multiply the pain.

Oh, how that cane punished. Oh, how I dreaded its continued application to my scalded seat.

How humiliated I was, too, standing naked in front of these two gorgeous feminine friends who were now enjoying my predicament. I couldn't bend over for any more, but I would have to if even a small part of my pride were to be left intact.

I was a grown man. Tens of thousands of young men over the years would have presented their arses for punishments like this and not come to any harm. But it hurt SO MUCH. I just couldn't have believed it.

"We are all still waiting," Olivia was saying. "Normally any disobedience, like you've just shown in getting up before I've given permission for you to do so, would result in my DOUBLING your punishment. However, as this is your first caning, we'll overlook this little interlude and carry on from where we got to, if you quickly bend over again. NOW, young man. NOW! Without further delay."

She swished the supple punishment cane through the air as she spoke, and then swiped it hard across the back of one of her armchairs. This produced an almighty THWHACK! as dust spurted out.

"Maybe the table would be better than the chaise longue," Jennifer suggested. "It would give him something to grip hold of, but he could still present his bare arse really well for us if he went up on tiptoe."

"Well spoken that woman!" said Olivia. "You heard what the doctor said, young man, so do it!"

My legs were shaking as I walked over to the table. I bent right over and pushed my bottom up and out like before.

I clung tightly to the far side and went up on tiptoe. Then I waited, breathing heavily, heart beating fast. In this completely new and even more exposed position, I was obviously displaying the result of Mrs Hamilton's initial efforts.

"What a perfect stroke!" Jennifer said, admiringly. "A beautiful stripe right across the middle of his seat, evenly marking both cheeks. That takes skill, Olivia. He's got a really magnificent arse," he added. "Two gorgeous, muscular mounds just crying out to be punished."

"Thank you, Jennifer," Olivia replied appreciatively. "I've watched a few canings over the years, as you can imagine. I've known a few guys who've produced nasty marks around the side, as it were, on young men's thighs. That's terrible. I NEVER do that. Accuracy is the whole thing with the cane."

"I wouldn't mind having a go myself," Jennifer murmured. "Do you think I could learn the technique? Young Daniel here has got a stunningly beautiful arse, as I say, and I think I'd enjoy caning it."

"If you are going to 'give', practice makes perfect." Olivia explained, while I stuck my bare, burning bottom in the air and waited, legs wide apart. I could feel the cool air going right into my crack so I knew my bum was wide open and exposed.

"I'm pleased to hear you might like to try caning, Jennifer. However, if you do decide to learn the technique, spend plenty of time caning a pillow or cushion before applying your cane to an adult male butt."

"An excellent idea," Jennifer replied. "And what else do I need to know? Where should I stand, for example?"

All this time I was displaying my bare bottom and nervously waiting. Olivia was in no hurry to deal with me, though. She was enjoying giving instructions to Jennifer.

"Stand well to the side and, in fact, stand a little forward of where you think you would stand. Poor technique will result in the right buttock being caned while the left one mostly escapes. The tip of your cane should be only just onto his right cheek, only just beyond his crack. Just a flick of the wrist is all it takes to give a stroke with a bouncing technique. Ready young man? Bottom right up! This stroke will truly sting!"

THWHACK!

The thin cane landed again, just a little lower and just a little harder. I yelled and then started involuntary gasping as the excruciating pain consumed me. I shook all over as my bottom started clenching and unclenching all by itself.

"Keep still!" Olivia commanded.

"Now, Jennifer. Watch this carefully. An even more painful stroke can be given by thwhacking the cane hard across the lower buttocks but not withdrawing it. The strokes so far have been bouncing ones. This time I shall make it land and stay there. Watch his reaction."

THWHACK!

Once again that cruel cane descended on its mission to inflict penetrating pain. It sank deep into my buttocks as Olivia demonstrated this different, even more painful technique. Wow did that hurt!

I cried out with all my might...

"Please Miss! NO MORE. Please Miss!"

Jennifer was addressing me now.

"Is that a more painful technique, young man? What's your opinion on the receiving end?"

"Oh yes, Dr Hargreaves! It's much more painful," I told her with tears in my eyes. "It hurts a lot more."

"I thought it probably did!" Jennifer answered, eyes lighting up.

The next three strokes were delivered at measured intervals, each one landing lower than the previous one. They all swiped across both of my exposed, quivering, meekly presented cheeks.

I cried out in agony as my bottom wriggled and writhed in a futile attempt to avoid each fresh onslaught. Is that really what misbehaving sixth formers would have experienced in days gone by?

No wonder manners were so good in those days. One visit to the Headmistress's study for six of the very best would have made absolutely sure you mended your ways. You wouldn't have wanted to return for a second dose.

(What was that Olivia had been saying about always making sure that regret was complete?)

Finally, I had received my first proper six searing strokes, and I had survived. I felt absolutely exhausted, but also pleased with myself.

"Do you have a birch, Olivia, and do you ever use it?" Jennifer asked.

"Yes, I do," Olivia said. "There are really two kinds of birches that can be used for corporal punishment, and I have one of each type which I keep standing in a bucket of brine. One is the spray birch consisting of a collection of very thin birch twigs about two foot six in length, bound together at one end with tape but splaying out at the other end so that they will cover a big area when swished across proffered bum-cheeks. The other kind is a similar collection of very fine canes, each wire-thin and extremely flexible, also about two foot six long and bound together at one end."

"I see," Jennifer replied. "And how do the effects compare?"

"In each case the effect is the same. I always birch bare buttocks. It is no use across pants or trousers. The stems spread out as they are thwhacked through the air and they sting like the very devil. While a school cane burns and stings in one fine line, either kind of birch will multiply the sting many times over and punish a wide area with each stroke. It will quickly cause unbearable pain all over the bare bottom being targeted and of course this builds and builds, more and more, as each stroke is applied over and over again on the same place."

"I guess you only use your birches on your more experienced subs?" Jennifer enquired.

Mrs Hamilton's answer was full, as usual.

"Well, it's something a man can progress to if he wants to achieve complete humility with me. However, if someone has misbehaved TOO much, I may decide that the birch is the only thing that will teach him the lesson he needs to learn. A guy who is used to being caned can quickly become very fearful when I bring out my birch."

I continued to stick my bottom up and out as far as I could while Jennifer sat well back in her chair and relaxed. She poured Olivia and herself more wine as she said

"If this young man were to report to you for a birching, what position would he have to adopt for you?"

"Good question," Olivia replied. "An ideal position for a birching is for the guy receiving to be made to kneel on the bed, legs wide apart. He puts his head right down on the sheet and his bare bottom then sticks up in the air just crying out to be birched! With his legs apart, his cheeks are spread wide open and of course his crack and arsehole are on show."

Again, Olivia was using words which wouldn't normally be those of a disciplinarian. What was her real motive? She carried on with her explanation.

"Not only is this extremely humiliating for him, but the birch twigs can easily be made to delve right in between his buttocks and punish the area a cane doesn't usually reach. This is his most sensitive and private area and I can assure you a birching which punishes his crack and hole will certainly make him think about misbehaving again!"

As I listened to all this, I realised that I'd been made to get into that position to be caned, and I found it made me feel completely vulnerable and exposed. My bottom was totally unprotected and, as Olivia was saying, my most private places were on show and being literally presented for punishment.

"It's the ideal position for receiving the cane or the birch," my new Mistress continued. "Equally good for either. The guy's most private places are being displayed, not for their own sakes but necessarily while he is waiting for punishment. What could be more humiliating?"

Jennifer wanted to know more about the difference between caning and birching.

"People tell me that the birch fell out of fashion in Victorian times, to be replaced with the cane. Why was that?" she asked.

"The Victorians introduced the cane because it could still hurt terribly through clothing, thus preserving the receiver's modesty while still causing him much pain and distress. They mostly stopped using the birch because it could only be used successfully on bare buttocks and they came to dislike this aspect. Obviously, this is not something I take into consideration when disciplining my regular adult pupils. Being naked and exposed only adds to the punishment."

Olivia Hamilton's reply was full and to the point, as always.

I found my cock beginning to harden again as I listened and waited increasingly nervously. I'd only had a few strokes of that terrible cane so far and I couldn't stop thinking about what was still to come.

Even though it filled me with dread, it made my manhood twitch and expand. I wanted to touch it but I couldn't. This only made it twitch and throb more.

The two female friends must have noticed that, surely?

Mrs Hamilton certainly didn't seem to have noticed as she continued

"I sometimes award both a caning AND a birching to a pupil. That way I can compare the reaction each one gets."

Jennifer changed the subject now.

"I've suddenly realised you've not given us a demonstration of spanking, Olivia. There's been all this caning and talk of birching, but no actual spanking so far."

Mrs Hamilton put her cane down carefully on the table and walked over to the sideboard. I remained with my now throbbing arse in the air while she poured herself a large gin and tonic.

"Will you join me, Jennifer?" she asked, bottle in hand.

"That's very kind of you," Jennifer replied. "Don't mind if I do. The wine is delicious but it's time we moved on to something stronger. How often do you give a spanking?"

"Most times a young man visits me," Olivia replied. She added ice cubes to Jennifer's glass and took it over to her.

"Many men I've had here for discipline think that a hand spanking is mild compared with the use of any implements, but they've always found my spankings surprisingly painful, and of course VERY embarrassing. What do you think, Daniel? Are you afraid of a spanking?"

"Not sure Miss," I said truthfully.

A spanking couldn't hurt more than the cane, surely, but it would certainly be more humiliating.

"Spanking can be deceptive," Olivia went on, "as, by its name, it seems a pretty mild option and, if you're a recipient of discipline, you're likely to think you've got off lightly if you're told you're just going to receive a hand spanking. Let me tell you, having spanked many men on their bare bottoms, a hand spanking from me is not a soft option."

"How do you give a spanking, Olivia?" Jennifer enquired, while my bottom flinched and twitched in dreaded anticipation.

"I'll give you an idea of the technique which as a giver you will certainly enjoy copying, Jennifer, or as a receiver you will certainly find very painful indeed. Obviously the first thing to be said about hand-spanking is that it should always be carried out on the bare bottom. There is little point in spanking a guy through trousers, and certainly not jeans! The initial spanking is best given over the knee, once the receiver has been made to take off his trousers and pants. I make him lay across my lap with his head down to the carpet and his bottom sticking right up."

Mrs Hamilton stopped at this point. I knew what was coming next. She sat down on a dining chair and beckoned to me.

"Come over here Daniel and get right over. Stick your bottom in the air for me. Then I can smack each cheek in turn."

While I reluctantly complied, Olivia waited until she was completely satisfied with my position. Then she addressed Jennifer.

"The secret is to vary the delivery after a while so that he doesn't know which cheek is going to get it next. Also, as the punishment progresses, the smacks should become both harder AND faster. I'll show you."

The spanking started. Olivia spanked HARD and quite FAST. She would choose a spot and concentrate on it for several spanks, smacking again and again, over and over on the very same increasingly tender spot, before moving a little to concentrate on another exposed and vulnerable area.

I blubbered and yelled out loud. I pleaded and begged for it to stop.

"Please Miss! I'll be good Miss! I promise Miss! Only please don't spank me any more Miss!"

Mrs Hamilton took no notice of my pleadings and merely chose another spot to punish. Bit by bit, she covered the whole of both of my tender cheeks with her relentless hard smacks.

Then she moved lower and started to spank the part where my bottom met the tops of my legs. Now that DID hurt!

Mrs Hamilton addressed Jennifer while she continued with her spanking and smacking.

"The recipient will always start to wriggle and/or clench his cheeks at this point," she explained "and this is when I tell him very firmly that if he doesn't keep still and keep his cheeks relaxed, I'll change to spanking him in the wheelbarrow position. Do you understand, young Daniel?""

"What's the wheelbarrow position?" Jennifer asked.

"That's where the receiver is face down in between the open legs of the giver who is sitting on the edge of the bed or sofa. I love giving prolonged, hard spankings in that position. The taker's face is right down on the carpet, his legs are spread wide open, one each side of my waist, and of course his bare bum is displayed right in front of me, in my lap. The fact that his legs are spread apart means that his bottom cheeks are spread wide and I can therefore start smacking the very sensitive parts in between."

I knew what was coming. After any number of faster, harder smacks, slaps and spanks had rained relentlessly down on my poor punished sit-upon I was suddenly told to get myself into the position that was known as the wheelbarrow.

This I eventually did, with a fair amount of explanation. It wasn't at all easy, but finally I was there, just as Olivia wanted me.

She continued with her commentary for Jennifer.

"An extra humiliation in this position is that the taker's arsehole is exposed and fully on show. It's also completely vulnerable and available for me to smack – like this - right there!"

"Ow! Please Miss! That hurts SO MUCH Miss!"

"Stop stating the obvious, Daniel," Olivia snapped. "Keep still for twenty-three more."

I'm hardly able to describe what happened next as my spanking continued. It was a complete blur. My world disappeared into a mass of pain and tears. Eventually I realised she had stopped.

I thought the cane had made me sore but now my arse was almost numb with the unbelievable relentless throbbing that Mrs Hamilton's skilful spanking had produced. She was an absolute expert in all forms of corporal punishment, that was for sure.

Once again, I was sent over to the corner to contemplate, hands on head. This time gave me the opportunity to think over what had just happened to me, and of course to think about what was still to come.

I knew better now than to let my hands stray to my butt. I was desperate to rub my cheeks but I managed to resist and meekly placed my hands together on the top of my head.

"You had 15 minutes of corner time just now, increased to thirty minutes because of your disobedience," Olivia announced. "In this instance, your corner time will be open ended. I will not allocate a specific amount of time. You will merely wait until I say I am ready to continue disciplining you. Jennifer and I are going to have our supper now, so it may be a long wait."

"Yes Miss," I replied disconsolately. What else could I say? I knew I mustn't argue or even discuss anything that my new Mistress decided. I was starting to learn what true discipline entailed. I clasped my hands together on the top of my head and waited … and waited.

As the time wore on, my hands began to feel increasingly numb. My arms were stretched upwards and were starting to ache also. Not aching as much as my arse!

Olivia and Jennifer were nearby all the time. They had placed their chairs on the other side of the old-fashioned dining table so that they could see me clearly in front of them.

One of Mrs Hamilton's methods, I was to subsequently learn, was always to monitor a pupil's corner time. This ensured that obedience was complete.

On a later visit I found to my cost the result of fidgeting and moving my hands away from my head merely to scratch an itch. I'd put them back again immediately, but Mrs Hamilton, quite rightly, pointed out that my behaviour was not as she had instructed and so I was then made to clench her favourite cane between the cheeks of my bottom as well as keeping my hands together on the top of my head.

My corner time was increased on that occasion by an extra 30 minutes and I was warned that I would receive six extra hard strokes of the cane if I didn't keep it tucked in between my buttocks. Very painful consequences would follow if I let it fall to the ground.

Boy, did I ache when she finally let me release it and put my hands down by my sides.

Olivia is just THE most wonderful disciplinarian.

At last supper time was over. I'd endured not only my extreme physical discomfort but also the mental torment of not knowing how long I was going to be there or knowing what further punishments awaited me that evening.

Now Olivia was behind me. She was gently removing her cane with one hand while she guided my hands down with the other.

"Hands down by your side," she said brightly.

During my prolonged corner time, the room had been filled with the enticing smell of beef casserole which Jennifer had remarked was "particularly tasty" apparently. Now the overriding aroma was of freshly brewed coffee emanating from a steaming cafetiere placed on a mat on the sideboard. Olivia guided me over to the low backed armchair with which I was becoming rather too familiar.

"Over you go again," she said, not unkindly as I bent right over, sticking my bruised, striped, agonised bum UP for her.

"You've done very well this evening, Daniel. I'm impressed with your performance here tonight. It certainly bodes well for future regular visits. You seem to me to be turning into an ideal pupil. I want to teach and you certainly seem to want to learn."

"Yes, I do Miss," I concurred, my voice mumbled as I spoke into the cushion. "And I do want to come for regular visits. No one has ever shown any care towards me before. You're the first, Miss, and I really do appreciate it."

"I know you do. I can see that," Olivia smiled. "Now, bottom right UP and legs as wide apart as they'll go. I shan't tell you again."

I complied with her instruction. Even though I was shaking with apprehension again, it felt good and my manhood's increasing stiffness acknowledged that.

"What were you thinking about during your last corner time, Daniel?" my Mistress enquired.

"Um, well ... I suppose I was thinking about how sore my arse was – er, bottom I mean, Miss ... and I was thinking about how much my arms and hands were aching as well. Oh, and I couldn't help thinking about how appetising your supper smelt. Also, I was definitely thinking about what was going to happen to me next. Whether you were going to cane me more, or whether I was going to be spanked – or something else, even. All that causes great apprehension and anxiety, Miss."

"I know it does. That's the idea. It's another excellent aspect of corporal punishment that people often overlook. It can be even more troubling than the pain of the punishments themselves."

"Yes Miss. I think it can, Miss."

"Quite. Well, you've been thorough in telling me your thoughts. However, there's one thought that you don't seem to have had. One of the purposes of corner time is to enable you to think over your misdeeds and connect them with the pain, discomfort and humiliation you are experiencing. In this way, the discipline achieves its objective. Your regret is, hopefully, complete and you decide to make absolutely sure you don't offend again in the same way."

"Oh, my regret is certainly complete, Miss," I assured her. "I've learnt my lesson now, well and truly Miss!"

Olivia took no notice of this remark and merely continued as if I hadn't spoken.

"Feeling the consequences in the form of your throbbing bum, your aching arms and your tormented mind, you tell yourself that if you commit the same misdeed again I will only punish you MORE severely. I'm sure you can see that would be the case, Daniel."

"Yes, I can Miss," I said, sticking my arse up even higher if that were possible. My cock was throbbing now, along with my buttocks, but in a different way!

Mrs Hamilton completed her explanation.

"This evening we have been dealing with your rudeness. You have another six strokes of the cane to come and then that should be sufficient to drive the message home that you will need to be polite and courteous in the future. More – a lot more – of what you've experienced here today awaits you if don't learn that particular lesson."

"Yes Miss."

"Next time you visit me, we will deal with your shocking treatment of your wife."

"Yes Miss. Yes please Miss."

"And then, on the third visit, I will punish you for your laziness and general lack of application. After that, I think you will be a different man. You will then visit me once a week just for regular discipline. I have a broad, comprehensive regime that I apply to the bare bottoms of several young men who visit me regularly. They all benefit greatly from my expert attentions and, of course, from time to time do commit particular offences that I then deal with by administering extra, what I call enhanced punishments."

"Yes Miss. Yes PLEASE Miss. Thank you very much Miss. You can enhance MY punishments any time you like Miss!"

CHAPTER SIX - EXTRA HUMILIATION

Olivia ignored that remark which was certainly a little cheeky – and also more than a little risky considering how much pain I had already suffered.

"So!" she said confidently, "now to your final caning for tonight, young man. You may like to come over here Jennifer to see this different technique from close range."

Jennifer left her chair and walked over nearer to where I was positioned, waiting, with my sore arse once more in the air. Meanwhile, Olivia spoke to me.

"Now Daniel, I'm going to give you six more strokes as I said, and they will all be hard ones. They will be applied rapidly, in quick succession, without any time in between to recover or to prepare yourself for the next. I've perfected this technique now, after lots of practice, and I know how to deliver each stroke just at the moment when the previous one has blossomed into its most intensely painful effect."

Yes Miss."

"I will also apply all six strokes very low down, right across your crease, just where your bottom meets the top of your legs. You'll feel these, Daniel! You will find them quite salutary."

"Yes Miss."

Mrs Hamilton was tapping. Very lightly she placed the thin, cruel cane just where it was going to land. I flinched and clenched my buttocks which were trembling in fearful anticipation.

"Don't clench! Relax your bum!" Olivia snapped impatiently.

I obeyed and then .... there was another ring at the door bell.

"Oh, I'd forgotten," Olivia said, gently putting the cane down on the table. "Stay where you are Daniel. My niece Laura is joining us."

My heart missed a beat and I broke out into a sweat.

She walked out of the room and along the corridor to the front door. I heard her letting in the extra guest and soon they both entered the room where I was obediently displaying my punished, striped, throbbing arse.

Laura could clearly see the results of the punishments I'd already had, and the position I was in obviously meant I was about to have more.

"Looks like I've come just at the right time, aunty," she said.

"Yes. Stand back. He's had a slow, thorough traditional caning, and been spanked as well. I'm just about to apply the final six to his bottom and these are going to be rapid ones. He knows that. I'd just explained this technique to him when you rang the bell."

Laura smiled as she walked over to stand next to Jennifer, where she could get a good vantage point.

Olivia picked up the cane and resumed the light tapping she'd started when we were interrupted. Then, suddenly ...

THWHACK!

THWHIPP!

THWHACK!

THWHIPP!

THWHACK!   ... and finally ...

THWHACK!

I let out a blood curdling yell.

"AAAAAAAAAARGH!

Ow! Ow! Ouch! Aaaaaaah! Oh, Miss! It hurts Miss! It hurts SO much Miss! I'm sorry Miss! I won't be rude again EVER Miss. I promise. Only don't cane me any more Miss. PLEASE Miss!"

Mrs Hamilton looked over at Laura and Jennifer, and smiled as she said

"I think we've achieved the desired result!"

She ran her fingers along the length of the thin supple cane that had achieved the result she referred to and placed it gently on the table where it waited in readiness for its next application to the meekly displayed buttocks of a regretful young man.

The cane's work done for now, it lay there peacefully until the next time it would be needed to inflict intense fiery pain with its harsh caress.

"You may stand up," she told me "and rub your bum as much as you like."

I rose gingerly and clutched my scorched, throbbing buttocks in a futile attempt to assuage the ferocious burning inferno within them. I just couldn't bring myself to look at Laura.

"Pull up your pants and trousers and make yourself decent again," Olivia instructed.

This was not easy to do as my buttocks only hurt more as the pants were pulled over them. When would I ever sit down again?

I was aware of the three adults looking not only at my exceptionally sore bum, but also at my raging erection which throbbed almost as much as my bottom. There was to be no relief for the moment and I merely had to tuck it away hoping for a chance to masturbate as soon as I possibly could.

"You can consider your rudeness dealt with completely," Olivia told me. "I will only ever deal with it again if there is a recurrence. In that case, as I'm sure you can imagine, I will be more severe than I have been today, and I'm sure you wouldn't want that. Bear that warning in mind young man, if you are ever tempted to be rude to me or anyone else."

"Oh, yes I will Miss," I assured her, still with tears in my eyes.

"Good," was all she said.

Then she added "My cane is always here, ready to inflict even more painful retribution to your most private areas if needed."

"Yes, I know that Miss," I replied meekly, looking at the slender crook-handled cane lying there, hardly able to believe what it was capable of doing.

Then I heard myself saying what I never would have thought I would.

"When should I report to you again Miss?"

Laura and Jennifer exchanged glances. Olivia waited a while before she replied. Eventually she said

"Are you sure that's what you want?"

"Yes I am, Miss," I said without a moment's hesitation. "No one has ever cared for me before, Miss, and I'm very grateful to you for giving your time to me."

"I can see that you are," my new Mistress smiled. "In that case, we'll make your visits weekly. Come back at the same time next Tuesday evening. We can review what we've achieved tonight and then we can go on from there to deal with your other misdemeanours one by one. You'll reap the benefits, I can assure you."

"Oh, I will Miss! Thank you, Miss. Thank you very much for disciplining me Miss." I said gratefully. "I know I will reap many benefits Miss."

"Complete humility – and I mean complete – is something I require from all my pupils and I think that seems to be something you are beginning to learn already. Well done, Daniel."

"Thank you, Miss.,"

"Very well then. We'll say goodnight and I'll look forward to seeing you again at the same time next week – and since we will be dealing with your treatment of your wife, next time you'll take the tawse as well as the cane."

I didn't actually know what a tawse was, but I just instinctively felt it would be something equally or more painful than the cane, and that it would be too much for me to cope with.

"Oh no Miss. Please Miss. I can't take the tawse as well," I pleaded.

Mrs Hamilton looked me straight in the eyes.

"If I say you will take the tawse, what will you do?"

"I'll take the tawse, Miss."

"Exactly."

"Yes Miss."

"Oh, and one more thing. I need to know the effect today's discipline has had, so that I can take you up a level next week. You are to report to me over the phone regarding your marks. A good, thorough traditional caning should produce marks that last three or four days. Ring me on Saturday morning to describe the appearance of your bottom then. I shall like to know whether the marks have faded completely or whether there's still some evidence to be seen that you've been caned."

I couldn't believe what I was hearing. This was an even more embarrassing humiliation for me to go through.

I was going to have to describe my bum in detail to this attractive, sexy woman over the phone. But there was more – much more. How could Olivia dream up these excruciatingly humiliating extras that would make her discipline regime more or less permanent?

"Obviously, we shall need a witness to verify what you are telling me. Do you live with anybody else?"

I blushed bright red and started to tremble again as I said "My flatmate Katy, Miss. She's just a flatmate. No more than that. We just live together to share the rent and the bills."

"How old is she?"

"Thirty-four, Miss."

"Excellent. She'll be around on Saturday morning no doubt?"

"Yes Miss."

"Very well then. Tell her about the phone call you are to make on Saturday and arrange for her to be present while you ring me. Once you've described your bottom to me, I'll speak to her just to verify that what you have said is true."

"But that means that she'll have to see my bare bottom too, Miss. I can't do that, Miss. I can't show her I've been caned."

"Yes you can, and yes you will. And I will remind you only this once that if you question my disciplinary decisions again, I shall impose an extra penalty."

I was going to plead with her but, looking into her eyes which were set coldly looking straight at me, I thought better of trying.

Olivia Hamilton's demeanour changed. She brightened up as she said

"Now, you've done very well indeed today, young man. Don't spoil this excellent start we've made. I'm sure you're already beginning to feel the benefits. That's something only you can experience and it's where you are the lucky one out of the three of us. Jennifer, Laura and I may well have enjoyed the evening, but we haven't got furiously burning bums. You'll enjoy a 'high' like you've never known before and we shan't get any of that. I think you know what I mean."

We shook hands warmly and I shook hands with Jennifer. Once out in the open air, I made my way back to my small flat with a new spring in my step.

Already the fire in my arse was beginning to turn into a deep heat which was extremely pleasant and satisfying. Huge numbers of endorphins were engulfing me and I don't know when I've ever felt such euphoria.

I felt so pleased with myself for having accepted the challenge of the discipline and got through it. I also felt as horny as hell.

The first thing I would do when I got back to my flat would be to masturbate. I would strip off completely, lie on my bed and then take my time to wank myself into an absolute frenzied stupor.... well, that's if I could make it last that long!

CHAPTER SEVEN – IN FRONT OF MY FLATMATE!

It was Thursday before I was able to explain my new situation to Katy. I'd agonised over how to do it more or less constantly since leaving Olivia and Jennifer. Then it happened all of a sudden and some of my explaining was already done for me.

I should tell you that, although I am straight, my flatmate Katy is only a friend. There's never been any problem between us, with one of us being a man and the other one being a woman.

I've known from the start that she likes and admires my butt. Although I say it myself, I've got a good physique. I'm a fine figure of a man. My narrow waist, broad shoulders and fine chest all look good.

My bum is very masculine, with muscular buttocks that are firm but still soft. When I wear smart, tailored trousers, they certainly fit well around my arse and really show it off. I know she loves looking at me as I walk around the flat.

Sometimes I bend over to pick something up just to tease her as she knows she can't do anything about her lust for me. We just don't "click" in that kind of a way. She's a very sexy woman, though. You can't deny that!

One thing I never do is walk around naked. Occasionally she'll see me in my briefs and I can tell that really gets her interested! Always, when I've had a shower, I go back to my room firmly wrapped in a towel.

On the Thursday following my visit to Mrs Hamilton, I was walking back to my bedroom from the shower, wrapped in my usual bright red towel. At the same moment, Katy came out of the living room towards the kitchen. As I avoided her, the towel slipped from around my waist and fell to the floor. I quickly bent down to pick it up but it was too late. Katy had seen my butt.

"Bloody hell!" she exclaimed. "What's happened to your arse, mate?"

I wrapped the towel back around my waist tightly.

By the morning of that day, the most vivid, intense stripes had faded, leaving a clear set of light marks all the way down my buttocks from just below the top of my crack to the very lowest part of my bottom, and onto the tops of my thighs. It was all a lot clearer on my right buttock but you could easily see the same effect on my left one, albeit a bit lighter.

Katy wasn't stupid. She could see I'd been caned.

Well, to cut a long story short, I told her about my rudeness to Olivia in the shop, my being sent to her house with a gift and an apology, my spotting the school cane in the hallway and her offer of discipline.

I didn't go as far as mentioning the fact that I had to phone her to describe my marks and the state of my bum. That was just TOO humiliating.

"You've got to admit, Katy, it's a fact that I've messed up big-time in my life," I said to her. "And Olivia Hamilton's really taking an interest in me. I mean, come to think of it, the fact that I'm sharing all this with you must mean that I'm starting to learn the humility she's trying to instil in me."

"I once played some spanking games with a guy I met," Katy confessed.

"You and your guys you've met!" I scorned. "How many is it now?"

"You're just jealous," she laughed.

"Yes, yes, yes," I snapped. "So, you've been spanked yourself?"

"Loads of times, but never the cane. I've thought about it, I must admit, but it would be just too bloody painful for me."

I could only agree that Mrs Hamilton's caning had been too bloody painful for me as well!

I told Katy that was the point. The cane is designed to hurt and Olivia had made my visit as painful as possible for me, in order to teach me the first of several lessons she said I needed to learn.

"Come on," she chided. "Let's have a closer look!"

"No way!" I shouted, clutching the towel tightly.

She tugged and tugged and it soon turned into a light-hearted chasing game with us both laughing and shouting. Eventually I said

"Oh, what the hell!"

I dropped the towel on the floor, turned around and bent over – just a bit.

Immediately, she was behind me, kneeling on the floor in fact, with her face level with my arse. She started to knead my cheeks lightly. Then she ran her fingers over my bum, just touching the hairs and barely touching my skin. It felt so good.

Next, she was running her fingers along the lines that were still clearly visible, tracing them along, and then letting her fingers go a little further just into my crack. My cock started to get hard. She certainly knew what she was doing, but then again maybe she'd had plenty of practice!

"A very sore bum!" she pronounced. "Beautifully striped I would say. Definitely the work of an expert."

I parted my legs to show her the cane effect more clearly.

She reached through between my open legs and lightly touched the back of my balls, again just teasing the hairs and not actually touching the skin. Wow! I'd never felt as horny as this.

I decided she'd gone far enough. I bent right down, picked up the towel and wrapped it firmly around me again, with my rock-hard cock now tenting it at the front.

"No more, I'm afraid," I said.

She looked crestfallen. "Not even a quick wank? I could do that for you right now if you like. Guys say I'm good at bringing them off. Sometimes quite slowly. I take them to the edge, you see, and then OVER the edge."

"Definitely not. There WILL be a wank, within about five minutes I should think, but it'll be on my own in my room. You make your own arrangements."

I started to walk away and then I remembered what else I had to tell her.

There was the question of the phone call I had to make. If I were to tell Katy about it, this was the moment – but it was just TOO embarrassing.

I stumbled over my words, and started again several times. Eventually she'd got the picture.

No one could have been more delighted to help than Katy. She would certainly be there while I rang Mrs Hamilton, and she would take great pleasure in speaking to her personally to confirm the state of my bum.

My humiliation was complete.

"Olivia Hamilton!"

"Oh, yes, good morning Miss. I'm ringing to report back Miss, as you told me."

"Good man. I knew you wouldn't renege on your agreement with me. You're going to be a very fine pupil. Is your flatmate there with you?"

"Yes Miss."

"What's her name?"

"Katy, Miss."

"And she's listening to all this?"

"Yes Miss."

"Fire away then, young man."

"Er .... um .... er ... what would you like to know Miss?"

"Good God, man. I thought I made that clear to you when you came to me on Tuesday. Don't waste my time or you'll be sorry on your next visit."

"Um ... yes Miss. Um ... er ... oh God ..."

Katy looked at me and smiled. She was so enjoying my acute discomfort.

"Um ... my bum is still marked quite clearly Miss. I've got stripes all the way down both cheeks, but they're clearer on my right buttock than on my left."

"That's only to be expected. The end of the cane lands on your right cheek and the tip of the cane always does the most work. How sore has your bottom been? Is it still difficult to sit down today?"

"Slightly, Miss. I can sit quite comfortably now if I lower myself down carefully, but it was very painful to sit down for the first couple of days, Miss. Now it's sort of fairly ok Miss."

"Right. Quite a reasonable, clear description. Part of the effect of a good caning is to ensure that you are reminded of your misdeeds every time you sit down for a nice long time after the punishment itself. It looks like we've achieved our aim."

"Yes Miss."

"And would you put Katy on now, please? I want to check that what you say is true."

"Yes Miss … Katy, she wants to speak to you."

I handed the receiver to my flatmate who immediately introduced herself.

"It's Katy here. Hi!"

"Good morning Katy. You've just heard what Daniel has told me. Is it true?"

"Oh yes. I've looked at his ass quite closely and it's definitely still well striped."

"Good. And did you witness him having difficulty sitting down a couple of days ago?"

"Yes, several times. I could tell he'd got a very sore butt. Not so bad now. The stripes still look great, though."

"Yes, I'm sure. You sound as though you like the appearance of a well-caned arse?"

"Oh yes, definitely Miss."

"I see. And would you enjoy SEEING an arse being expertly caned?"

Katy's eyes lit up. "Absolutely Miss!"

"Then may I suggest that you accompany young Daniel on his next visit to my study. I'm going to introduce him to the tawse before he receives his next caning. Would you like to watch all that?"

"You bet I would. I'd absolutely love it Miss!"

"I thought so. See you on Tuesday then. And explain our little arrangement to Daniel, won't you?

He'll be so apprehensive if he knows what's planned!"

Mrs Hamilton chuckled as she put the phone down.

There was no need for Katy to explain anything to me. I'd heard the whole conversation from both sides as our phone had a speaker phone which I'd activated before Katy took over.

What could I say? It wasn't for me to argue or question anything. I was under Mrs Hamilton's discipline – permanently now it seemed – and this was another part of it I would have to get used to.

Tuesday evening arrived all too quickly. I showered and shaved and Katy did the same. We walked in silence down the village street to the neat, well ordered house that was to be my regular port of call on a Tuesday evening.

Olivia was welcoming but the formalities were brief. Soon I'd stripped off completely and knelt up on a couch that was probably specially kept for the purpose. I stuck my head down and my bare bottom up, parted my legs wide and presented my still striped arse for Olivia and my flatmate Katy to view.

"Mmmmmm. A very good result from a first visit, although I say it myself. Some very nice stripes, evenly placed all the way down both cheeks. Clearer on the right. Nearly completely faded on the left. Excellent! Now today, we're going to deal with your treatment of your ex-wife. Remind Katy what we dealt with last week, please."

I hesitated, blushed bright red and still stuck my arse right UP in the air as I said

"My rudeness, Miss."

"And what did we do to rectify it? What did you get?"

"I got the cane Miss."

"Exactly. And today, you'll get the cane again. However, the way you treated your wife is far more serious that just rudeness and we will deal with it accordingly. I've decided to use the tawse to help you remember to treat people well. And then I'll use my favourite cane to make sure we really drive the lesson home."

Just like the previous week, I started to panic. Olivia had a way of making the dialogue as big a part of the discipline as the painful punishments themselves."

"I'm afraid I don't know what a tawse is, Miss," I had to admit.

"I admire your honesty Daniel. The tawse is an excellent Scottish tradition, sadly dying out now. It's a thick leather strap, especially made for punishing young men's hands or bare buttocks. Obviously, a leather strap hurts tremendously if thwhacked hard across outstretched palms or well-presented buttocks."

"Yes, I'm sure it does Miss."

"The cunning thing about the tawse, though, is its clever design which increases the pain several times over. It's a thick leather strap which is cut into either two or three tails, as they're called, so that each stroke is doubled or tripled. The edges of the tails are particularly painful and the leather is thick enough to make a real impact along the length of each tail as well."

What could I possibly say but "Yes Miss"?

"You'll find the tawse over there in the top drawer, Katy. Bring it to me, would you?"

Katy walked over to the tall old-fashioned chest of drawers. She took the tawse from the drawer and ran her young, feminine hands along its length, feeling its weight.

Katy spoke up as she handled the three-tailed tormentor which I would soon be learning my next lesson from.

"You mentioned hands and buttocks, Mrs Hamilton. Which area was it usually used on? I think both places would soon hurt a lot after just a few strokes. This tawse of yours is a beauty. Quite heavy to hold and well balanced."

Olivia Hamilton's reply was thorough as usual.

"Many people think the tawse is best given on the hands. It's certainly a very good Scottish tradition as I said. Having to hold your hands out in turn to have them painfully tawsed is a particularly humiliating punishment as you have to be a willing part of causing your own hurt and discomfort by meekly holding your hand out, palm up."

"That must be quite difficult to do," Katy mused.

"Yes, it IS quite difficult to do, knowing how much it's going to hurt when those leather thongs or fingers smack down. All part of the complete humility you have to learn to show me, Daniel."

Katy enquired further, while still lovingly stroking the tawse along the length of its three cleverly designed tails. "You mentioned a Scottish tradition. How was it given in days gone by?"

"The time-honoured way to give the tawse is always to deal with alternate hands. The recipient has to hold out one hand, have it smacked with the leather tawse, then change over hands to have the other one punished. Of course, the hard part comes when it's time to hold the first hand out again while it's glowing and stinging so much from the first blow."

"That must be almost impossible to do," Katy said.

"Yes. The second stroke will hurt more, given that it lands across an already burning hand. Obviously, the hands must be changed over again for the other hand to be punished for the second time. Three strokes on each hand is the norm. And the third stroke is going to hurt a great deal – as I'm sure you're imagining, Daniel."

"Yes, I can imagine," Katy mused. "So, I'm sure Daniel can imagine the effect as well!"

"It really is very difficult to voluntarily proffer your hands for the third time when you've just discovered what a painful tawsing entails!

However, with me, no amount of begging or pleading will be listened to and the third and most memorable part of the punishment will be carried out without question. This will probably result in the recipient squeezing his burning hands under his armpits in a futile attempt to dull the pain."

My flatmate Katy blushed bright red while hearing the lurid descriptions of painful punishments so enthusiastically spoken about.

"Wow! It's almost hurting me just hearing about that," she said. "I guess a hard tawsing like you've just described would be a pretty painful grand finale to a punishment session with you, Miss."

I wasn't sure why Katy called Olivia "Miss", but it was hardly surprising, even though Katy was not going to have to submit herself.

Mrs Hamilton laughed as she said, "Grand finale? On the contrary. I often find that my male pupils, no matter whether they're young men, middle aged or whatever, can never take one of my hand tawsings without a lot of pleading, yelping, etc. This will usually result in extra discipline after the tawsing has been completed to my satisfaction. Daniel has come to me to learn TOTAL humility as I've said, and with me, extra punishment is always called for if there is any kind of protest or pleading."

Katy was incredulous.

"EXTRA punishment? Really?"

"Yes, an ideal extra punishment to give immediately after a hand-tawsing is a hundred lines. I just watch the guy's face when I tell him to sit down and write a full one hundred times 'I must learn total obedience and complete humility through really hard hand-tawsing in order to improve my performance and behaviour to Mrs Hamilton's entire satisfaction'."

I started to tremble as I heard this. I'd resigned myself to receiving the tawse, and told myself that it couldn't possibly be as bad as the cane, but now I wasn't so sure I'd be able to get through it without this extra indignity.

Olivia hadn't finished, though.

"When writing lines for me, attention must be paid to spelling, and of course extremely neat and tidy handwriting is essential – which is difficult if your hand is stinging and shaking as it undoubtedly will be after I've applied my thick leather tawse vigorously to your palms and fingers. However, if you are to avoid another tawsing, you will soon learn you'll have to write neatly for me."

The more the conversation was prolonged, the more nervous I became about submitting to the Scottish tawse. Katy asked the next question.

"You've spoken only of tawsing a guy's hands so far. Do you ever apply it to men's bottoms? You said that this was also done, traditionally."

"Yes of course. It's more satisfying for me because I enjoy seeing the different marks I can create with the tawse. They're not the same as cane stripes, obviously. And then a guy's reaction to the tawse is different too, as I expect we shall shortly see with Daniel here today."

"How is the reaction different?"

"It can be even more vocal than during a caning. Tawsing a guy's bottom is best carried out 'on the bare' so that the giver can see the effect they are having. Two or three tails will create beautiful clear marks, forming an attractive pattern across both buttocks. The tips of the tails hurt the most, and will cause the deepest marks. With this in mind, care should always be taken to apply the tawse so that the tips are only just onto the further cheek – as in caning. This way, there will be no wraparound and if the guy who's been misbehaving bends right over with his cheeks spread well apart, the tips of the tails will sometimes go right down into his crack and land right on his exposed arse hole."

Hearing all this being explained to my female flatmate, I was barely able to continue sticking my bottom up, waiting for my torment to begin.

Katy was amused and intrigued. "Is that what's going to happen to Daniel today?" she asked, brightly with quite a gleam in her eye.

"It may well do," Olivia replied casually. "During my tawsings, those wicked tails often seem to find their way deep into the private area in between the buttocks. That usually gets a loud response, and, of course, that's all to the good because it tells me my punishment is having the desired effect and my discipline is working."

Katy walked around to the front of where I was waiting in position, looked me straight in the eyes and grinned.

Mrs Hamilton suddenly announced that the discussion was over and the practical demonstration was about to begin.

"Right! We'll make a start I think. I'm going to tawse your bum today and we'll keep your hands for another time – unless there's any disobedience, that is. I'll remind you that you have agreed to this discipline. In fact, you have actually asked me for it. You have attended voluntarily this evening so if you start crying out 'Please Miss, no more Miss, it hurts too much Miss!' I'll merely continue. Everything is consensual between us. Everything is safe, and at all times, common sense prevails."

With that, she picked up the long, heavy tawse and flicked it lightly against her hand. I felt I had to reply, even though my head was down in the cushions, and all I could possibly say in the circumstances was "Yes Miss."

"Now let's have that bottom a little higher for its punishment", Olivia instructed. I was already humiliatingly positioned in front of my feminine flatmate with my bare arse displayed pretty high, but this was not enough for her.

I strained to comply.

"Part your legs more – really wide." Olivia commanded.

"Why do you want his legs so far apart?" Katy asked." What difference does it make?"

"So, my tawse can sting Daniel's most sensitive parts of all", Olivia explained.

"Yes of course," Katy agreed.

"The insides of his cheeks are a little softer that the main part of his buttocks, so the tawse will have more effect if he exposes that area to me. The tails are bound to go right down into his crack a few times and he'll really feel that, I can assure you! Also, of course, presenting those most private areas for punishment is particularly humiliating, thereby increasing the overall effect of the discipline."

"You really are an expert," Katy chuckled admiringly. "I hope Daniel is grateful for all the trouble you're taking."

"I'm sure he is. Aren't you, Daniel?" Olivia laughed.

Once again, all I could say in the circumstances was "Yes Miss. I AM grateful Miss. Very grateful indeed Miss."

"What are you?" she asked, a little more menacingly this time.

"Grateful Miss," I replied, with my head down and bottom up and waiting.

"Grateful for what?" she snapped.

I felt obliged to give a fuller answer. "I'm grateful for your excellent discipline, Miss, and all the trouble you're taking to punish me completely."

As I said this, I was aware of a definite stirring in my nether regions, and my cock started to come to life of its own accord. I didn't dare touch it. I just stuck my ass up further, and patiently waited.

Then it started.

THWHACK!

With a vicious swipe, Olivia aimed the tawse and brought it right down hard across the very middle of my arse, stinging both of my exposed cheeks but, as she had said it would, having a much greater effect on my right buttock.

"Keep your bottom HIGH for me or I shall add extra strokes for disobedience," Olivia said loudly. "I'm really going to make your buttocks bounce now, young man."

And she did.

Time and again that wicked tawse thwhacked across my poor, sore sit-upon, landing over and over with increasing severity and frequently going right into my exposed, meekly presented crack.

Each time it did so, those terrible tails did their work right on my hole and just around it. My crack is a little more hairy than my buttocks and the area where the hairs grow is particularly tender. Mrs Hamilton's thick, heavy tawse found those areas again and again until the whole of the inside of my crack was bright red and very sore. Not that she forgot to punish my cheeks as well.

"If you thought a tawsing was a soft option, you'll soon find out it's not," she told me, thwhacking away enthusiastically while Katy looked on in awe.

"You'll soon discover the way that I use the tawse really hurts," she announced brightly.

I had already discovered that from the very first stroke.

"These next six harder strokes will remind you of your disgraceful treatment of your wife and teach you to treat other people well at all times," she said. "My tawsings always sting, as you are finding out!"

As my first ever tawsing progressed, I couldn't help crying out "Ow Miss! Please Miss! I can't take any more Miss! I promise I'll be good Miss … only it hurts so much Miss!"

Like during my caning the previous week, this had no effect on Mrs Hamilton's technique. She merely carried on in the very same way, in the regular rhythm she had established, inflicting more and more pain with each thwhack.

"It's MEANT to hurt! That's the whole idea. Now get your bottom up higher and I'll continue."

Twenty minutes later, I was back in the corner with my hands on my head, my bright red glowing arse on show and my manhood starting once again to rise and expand.

As I stood, waiting, embarrassed but increasingly horny, there was another surprise in store for me.

Mrs Hamilton and Katy were enjoying a leisurely cup of coffee and a few chocolate biscuits. I think Katy must have been as surprised as I was to hear what Olivia was planning next for me.

"He's got his caning to come, as you know Katy. How would you feel about spanking him yourself before he gets the cane? I always believe every discipline session should be really thorough."

"Me?" Katy was incredulous.

"Yes you. He's starting to learn humility as you can see. He doesn't question any of my methods now. He just takes whatever I decide to give and he doesn't complain when his arse burns like fire. He's just obediently waiting for more right now, isn't he?"

"Well, yes," Katy agreed.

"There will be extra humiliation for him if YOU spank him. Going over a young lady's knee – especially a young lady who shares his flat with him and knows him pretty well - he'll learn more humility, which is what I want. I'd get you to cane him, but that requires great skill which few people have and I wouldn't risk it. I never want to do him any harm. I've promised that to him and an inexperienced amateur like you with a cane in her hand is going to be flailing about all over the place. However, if you spank him soundly, you can't possibly do him any harm. Just warm his bottom for him. Make it even hotter than it already is! Does that sound enjoyable?'"

In the corner, facing the wall I listened in horror – but my cock had its own agenda. It rose quickly to stand out firm and proud, twitching slightly as I thought about going over my attractive flatmate's knee to be spanked.

"A great idea and very well put," Katy announced. She turned to me.

"Right young man, normally I'd say let's have your trousers and pants down, but they already are. So! I'm going to spank you, and then Olivia is going to give you a really thorough caning. Come and get over my knee. Head right down. Bottom right up!"

I meekly walked over to Katy and arranged myself over her lap so that my incredibly sore butt was right where she wanted it.

I parted my legs wide and placed my two hands firmly on the carpet in front of me and waited. I didn't have long to wait.

Smack, smack, slap, splat, smack, smack. Her spanking was hard right from the beginning.

I wriggled and squirmed in a vain attempt to move my sore bum away from the target area. "Oh, please Katy. I won't do it again," I cried desperately. I was now begging my flatmate not to smack me so hard! I couldn't believe it – but her spanking hurt so much.

"If there's any more argument from you. I'll DOUBLE the punishment," she announced. "Now get those legs wider apart and bend right down over my knee."

Spank, smack, smack, slap, slap...

After a while, I was really starting to struggle and wriggle.

"Aaah! Oh, Miss! Tell her to stop, please Miss! I'll be good Miss!"

"Yes, you will! AFTER I've spanked you, and Olivia has caned you," Katy told me firmly.

"But it hurts so much. No more please Katy!"

"I know it hurts. That's the whole idea." Katy was really getting into the swing of the spanking, and thoroughly enjoying herself. "I'll decide when you've had enough. Now keep your bottom still while I smack harder."

"Aaah! Ow! Ouch! Ooooh!"

"Good! I'm glad to hear I'm getting through to you. And don't forget you've got your caning to come!"

In complete distress and despair, I called out again to Mrs Hamilton. "Aaaaah! Please Miss! There's no need to cane me after this, Miss! I've learnt my lesson Miss, really I have!"

Her reply was firm and to the point.

"I DO need to cane you, to make sure you learn your lesson. First, however, I think ten or twenty minutes in the corner after your spanking will help you focus your mind. It'll give you time to think about your caning to come, and remember how much my canings always hurt. Remember also that this whole evening is to punish you for the way you treated your wife."

Dialogue like this can multiply a session in intensity several times over. When she said that, my attitude changed.

I accepted I DID need to be punished. I stuck my bottom up, gritted my teeth and thought how sorry I was for what I had done while the harder and harder slaps rained down on my poor defenceless bottom.

Eventually Katy stopped and I was sent gasping and blubbering to the corner once again. Just ten or twenty minutes was the allocation this time, and throughout it, Olivia could be heard swishing the cane through the air and occasionally thwhacking it down hard across the back of the sofa. Soon it would be thwhacking hard across my bum. I didn't know whether I would be standing there for ten minutes or twenty – but soon the waiting time was over in any case.

Back to Olivia I went for MORE discipline!

The caning was severe. It consisted of six hard, accurate strokes delivered systematically all the way down my bare buttocks from the middle to the tops of my thighs.

There are no words to describe the amount of pain and distress Olivia Hamilton's favourite cane caused.

At the end of the six strokes I knew I was completely contrite. I'd decided never ever again to be unkind to my wife, a future girlfriend – or indeed anyone. The cane always produces results. It never fails to change behaviour for the better.

If only Sixth Forms and Colleges understood this simple fact and put it into practice. Highly unlikely in this wishy-washy society where bad manners, foul language and downright insolence reign completely unchallenged.

Eventually it was time to dress, to shake Mrs Hamilton's hand and thank her.

"Don't forget to thank young Katy here," she said. "She did a very good job I thought. Don't you agree?"

"Yes she did, Miss," I concurred. "Thank you, Katy." I shook her hand and she shook mine warmly. I really was starting to learn the complete humility Olivia required. "Any time, mate," she grinned.

On the Saturday, another phone call took place in which I had to describe my bum and tell my Mistress how much it had ached and for how long. The tawse and the cane combined had produced a different, more intense effect than the caning alone the previous week and Olivia was pleased to hear this.

Katy was called upon once again to verify the state of my arse and this she did with great relish while I pulled my pants down for her. She knelt down behind me to see it and feel it while she spoke over the phone.

My next appointment was made for the following Tuesday on which occasion Olivia had said she would deal with my general laziness and lack of application. Katy was to accompany me once again.

CHAPTER EIGHT – A TIME-HONOURED BRITISH TRADITION

"Ah! My new young charge and his flatmate friend! Come in, please. How nice to see you both." Olivia welcomed us warmly and led us through to her study – for my third time and Katy's second.

"Take off all your clothes," she instructed me, "and while you are doing so, you can remind us all why you are here."

I struggled out of my top layers while she and Katy watched. Did she mean I was to rehearse the misdemeanour which was to be dealt with today? Olivia seemed to have a predilection for using lewd words as well as the cane, so I decided to go down this route. I'd got down to just my skimpy pants as I said

"To have my arse caned, Miss."

I hoped this was the kind of remark she wanted to hear.

"Is that wishful thinking on your part?" she enquired menacingly.

"No Miss."

"What is it that makes you think that only your arse will suffer? I distinctly remember making it clear to you that I also cane hands if I feel it appropriate to do so."

"Yes Miss."

"Your remark strikes me as impertinent, therefore. You appear to be trying to limit what is going to happen to you. You have also deliberately used a rather obscene word. I am the one who will decide whether it's your arse or your hands – or both - that will be punished this time. You were pushing your luck, weren't you?"

"Oh no Miss. I didn't mean to do that, Miss."

I pulled my thin cotton briefs down, letting my manhood spring up in front."

"May I suggest that you correct your remark right away, in order to avoid any possible misunderstanding?"

"Yes Miss. Thank you Miss. I am here to have the cane, amongst other possible punishments as you see fit, and to take it across my bare buttocks and/or my hands, Miss."

"Exactly. Well put. Now Katy, please place his pants over there on the back of the sofa."

Full of embarrassment already, I handed my pants to my feminine flatmate.

Once I had stripped completely, I was told to kneel up on the couch again and present my bottom firstly for inspection. Plenty of nice, raised red marks were still in evidence all over my soft cheeks. Olivia ran her fingers along the slight ridges that remained and pressed the flesh of my buttocks.

"Clearly showing the results of a good, thorough caning. A time-honoured British tradition!"

"Yes Miss." On hearing this, I stuck my bottom UP and OUT, as far as it would go.

"I need to examine the area in between," she said. As she spoke, she opened up my crack with her fingers to see if the effect of the tawsing was still in evidence.

"Mmmmmm. Still a bit of reddening in here," she mused. "Has this been a sore area during the week?"

"Yes Miss."

"And it's felt different from how it usually feels?"

"Yes Miss." I started to squirm in embarrassment.

"On both sides of your crack, or just the one?"

"Both sides Miss. Possibly a bit more on the right side Miss."

"Yes, well, that's only to be expected as I discipline from the left. And your arse hole?"

There was a long pause before I could speak.

"It's been very sore Miss."

"So, that's felt different from how it usually feels also?"

"Yes Miss."

"Good. All of that has been a constant reminder to you during the week that you've been punished?"

"Yes Miss."

"And you've kept in mind WHAT you were punished for?"

"For the way I treated my wife, Miss."

"Exactly. So, our methods have good results."

"Yes Miss. Very much so, Miss."

"Remain in position while I explain what we're going to do today. I'm going to give you another caning at the end, as that is the most effective discipline I know, but I like to ring the changes also."

"Yes Miss."

"You will therefore receive another spanking from Katy first. She showed good technique last week, wouldn't you agree?"

"Oh yes Miss. Yes, I would agree Miss. Definitely, Miss," I replied, bottom in the air, cock standing to attention.

"Very well. Katy, I'm going to ask you to take your spanking technique a stage further. How do you feel about using the slipper today?"

Katy's eyes lit up as she said enthusiastically "Oh yes, I'd love to give that a go Miss. I think I could do it really well Miss. The slipper was often used as a punishment in the past, wasn't it? Do you recommend it yourself?"

"Yes, of course. It's completely different from the cane which is undoubtedly my favourite to use. It smacks, rather than slices like the cane, so it makes a sort of 'splat' sound as it lands on bare buttocks. Being rather regressive, it seems to embarrass my pupils more."

"Yes I see," Katy said. "So how do you give the slipper?"

I remained motionless in position while this was explained.

"If I decide to give a slippering, I still make sure it's as painful as possible in order to drive the lesson home. It doesn't hurt as much as the cane (nothing does except perhaps the birch) but it can be really painful in a different way. It will cover quite a large area with each stroke, and after about 20 or 30 vigorously applied slaps, can usually quite quickly reduce the recipient to pleading and begging for it to stop."

"I'll see if I can do that," Katy said enthusiastically.

"Good. I make sure I cover the whole of both cheeks and the tops of both thighs so that there's a healthy rosy glow all over when I've finished. The misbehaving man's bottom will always be really hot to the touch after one of my memorable slipperings."

"Wow!" Katy was impressed, and once again my manhood proved it had a mind of its own. It rose to a firm, throbbing erection which, of course, I was able to do nothing about.

Katy warmed to the subject under discussion and showed a surprising knowledge.

"What about the wooden or leather paddle?" she asked. "How effective is that, in comparison to the slipper?"

"Americans are very fond of the paddle for corporal punishment." Olivia replied. "They mostly use wooden paddles, either smooth or drilled with several holes. The holes increase the effect – that's why they're there."

Even though I was obediently presenting my wide-open bottom all this time, I summoned the courage to ask the next question myself.

"How do the holes increase the effect, Miss?" I ventured.

"Sensible of you to ask. A hard wood paddling is extremely painful anyway, but the addition of several holes increases the velocity of each stroke as the air resistance is reduced. The edges of the holes themselves also hurt in their own extra way, probably doubling the pain at the very least. A cunning and clever idea by whoever thought of it, and well worth the effort of drilling the holes for the increased effect you will achieve."

"Do you have a paddle?" Katy asked inquisitively.

"Yes, of course. I have two. One smooth hardwood, and one drilled with eight holes. You really know you've had that one!"

Katy continued with her questions.

"The hairbrush or bath brush is said to be particularly painful, isn't it? Do you recommend either of them?"

"They are both excellent punishment implements. The hairbrush is usually oval and the bath brush is usually round, but they have the same effect. Being small, they pack a real punch without much effort on the part of the giver. This is an obvious advantage as you can give a good, long, thorough hairbrushing without tiring yourself unnecessarily."

"Which are you thinking of me using on Daniel today Miss?"

"All three. The slipper, the paddle and the hairbrush. A few minutes with each will make a good firm start to the evening, and then after some corner time, Daniel can bend over for a good, hard, traditional caning to send him on his way!"

"A very good plan!" Katy replied.

I was made to walk over to my attractive young flatmate once again and place myself over her knee. I was told to get myself into position so that my bottom was best placed for Katy's smacks.

She picked up Mrs Hamilton's slipper and began. She smacked hard and then she smacked harder. As I'd heard, it was a very different effect from that of the cane. I can't say if it was as painful or more painful. It was just different.

Each hard smack covered a surprisingly big area and my cheeks flinched and writhed in agony as stroke after stroke of that flexible rubber-soled slipper rained down onto my soft, unprotected bum.

"Ah! Ow! Ouch! Oh no! Please! AAAAH!"

My cries were to no avail.

Olivia Hamilton had placed a kitchen timer by Katy's side and set it for a full three minutes of torment. You wouldn't believe how many smacks I got in just those three minutes. (You just try it and you'll see what I mean.)

I gasped and wriggled, clenched and unclenched my buttocks but the hard, painful slippering went on and on until the bell rang to end my humiliating torment.

Ten minutes' corner time were soon over and I was back over Katy's knee for the paddle.

Since I was to receive just three minutes' paddling (and that would be MORE than enough), Katy was told she could choose which of Mrs Hamilton's two paddles she would like to use. As I'm sure you can guess, she chose the one with the eight holes.

Words can't describe how much that terrible paddle hurt.

The holes doubled the effect, like Olivia had said, and I was so grateful when the three minutes were up as I was sure the edges of the holes were starting to cause blisters. My erection was long gone. It had disappeared as soon as the paddling began and I became increasingly vocal, and increasingly desperate as it progressed.

When it was over, I managed to tentatively and politely ask Olivia if I'd got blisters on my bum-cheeks from the edges of those wicked holes.

"Let's have a close look," she said, bending down to get her head next to my agonised, throbbing arse. She ran her hands over my cheeks and then patted me brightly.

"You're quite right to ask," she said, not unkindly. "I've promised we'll never do you any harm and I will always keep to my word. You've got a very healthy, rosy glow – but no blisters. Katy is doing a very good job. The hairbrush to follow hasn't got any holes so there won't be any blisters from that. It's just the size of it that needs to concern you."

"Yes Miss."

"Think about the very small area in which all the pain will be concentrated. Each stroke is memorable in itself, but if Katy chooses an area and then concentrates on it for quite a while before moving elsewhere, you'll find the effect just about completely intolerable – but memorable nonetheless, which is the whole idea."

Katy spoke up as I painfully got up and walked over once again to the corner with which I was becoming so familiar by now.

"Corner time or waiting time!" Katy said. "I'm beginning to see the advantages."

"Yes, absolutely," Olivia said as I placed my hands on my head, my legs apart and my nose against the wall. "He's only had basic corner time so far, but of course if there's any real disobedience, there's also what I call 'holding uncomfortable positions'."

"What do you mean?" Katy asked.

"Well, I'm sure Daniel here won't be disobedient this evening, but some of my pupils are not so compliant. For those who mistakenly think they can disobey me, I often impose the added indignity of uncomfortable corner time. VERY uncomfortable indeed!"

I panicked as she said this.

"Such as?" Katy enquired.

"Well, my favourite is to make a disobedient pupil hold the cane ready for me to punish him with. The ten minutes' corner time is spent in the corner but facing outwards, both arms outstretched in front. I place the cane resting across the two arms about halfway along the forearms. You have to stay very still or you will drop the cane. If this happens, I give your arms six quick sharp strokes with it and then replace it to be balanced again, this time for twenty minutes. Your arms soon start to ache – and of course, this is the idea, to teach you that disobedience always has a consequence."

"You think of everything, don't you Miss?" Katy said admiringly.

"I try to," Olivia replied. "But we won't need to use that technique with young Daniel here tonight. He's a very good man, here to learn, and he's determined to get the best out of each of his painful sessions with me. I'm very pleased with him."

After what seemed a very long time in the corner – but was actually quite short - I was back over Katy's knee for the hairbrush.

Katy remembered the advice she'd been given, and right from the start she would choose a spot to concentrate on and whack it over and over again with that cruel, hard little wooden brush.

How I howled and pleaded. How I begged for it to stop, but nothing deterred my determined flatmate. She smacked and smacked away with gusto until my bum-cheeks were both a bright cherry red and so hot to the touch that you'd think they were on fire.

When the bell rang to indicate my three minutes were up, all Katy did was casually enquire whether Olivia had any other wicked disciplinary techniques up her sleeve.

"Well," she said. "There are lots. As well as the actual pain caused by the spanking, caning or whatever, there are unpleasant things like embarrassment in front of friends or strangers, writing lines or impositions, and as I've said before a good disciplinarian always adds additional punishments for disobedience – enemas, chastity amongst other things."

Katy was fascinated. "Chastity?" she asked. "How do you achieve that with a grown man?"

"I'm a great believer in chastity for my subs," Olivia replied, while I quaked in horror. The one thing that was enabling me to get through this terrible, rigorous, relentless discipline regime was the fact that I could wank myself silly after each visit. What if that were somehow prevented?

"Chastity is an excellent extra discipline for my submissive men. It helps them to learn total humility, obedience and submission. I have a number of superb male chastity devices which all do the trick very effectively. They vary in design. Some are clear plastic and some are metal. They all have the same effect, however, and that's to prevent you from touching your penis. No matter how aroused it gets, it can't get completely hard. You can never masturbate, so of course, you can never shoot your load while it's on."

Katy and I were both completely gobsmacked. Neither of us spoke for some while, until Katy managed to ask the obvious.

"How does it work Miss?"

"It's very clever. A ring encloses the balls which hang through in front of it, and a hard, rigid tube which points downwards, encases the penis firmly, locked out of reach. It can be seen but not touched. And of course, most certainly not masturbated or 'wanked' as young Daniel here would probably say. Your cock is trapped, pointing down and there's no way it can get erect. The Mistress has complete control as she holds the key and is the one who decides if and when the sub's cock will be released. It's not possible to shoot your load while you're locked in chastity, as I said, so it can be extremely frustrating. Just imagine how horny a young man would get if his cock was prevented from shooting its load day after day after day!"

"Wow!" Katy was clearly excited.

I was terrified.

"Is chastity a normal part of your discipline for all your guys?" Katy asked, while I started to shake nervously.

"I use it as an extra punishment for real disobedience. And only after a warning that it will be used."

I made up my mind then and there to always obey Olivia without question.

"If I decide it is called for, it will last a couple of weeks. Six days locked. One day unlocked. Then six days locked again and one final day unlocked at the end. After that I find my men are always completely compliant. On the final day unlocked, we always discuss whether the technique has been effective and whether the guy would benefit from a longer period. Always, the answer is a resounding no, pleading with me to never lock him again. I, however, remind the young man that a chastity device is always waiting for him if he seriously disobeys me. That certainly concentrates the mind!"

I was the one who asked the next question. I suppose I sounded naïve, but I couldn't see what would happen if you started to get an erection.

"What happens if your cock starts to get hard inside the device, Miss?" I enquired nervously.

"As it always does," Olivia concurred. "There's room for expansion certainly, but not room for a full erection. The penis will therefore grow a bit and start to throb, but remain completely frustrated. The hard cock cage points resolutely downwards, as I said. It therefore keeps your cock pointing downwards and unable to rise. There's no chance for relief until your cock is released after the six days."

"With your cock caged like that for several days, isn't there a problem with cleanliness?" Katy asked.

"Not at all. There's no worry about hygiene. The cages all have plenty of holes for cleanliness. You have to keep your cock clean by playing the shower onto it through the holes. Unfortunately, this is stimulating in itself so this will always result in an even more desperate attempt at an erection – which is, of course impossible as I have the key. Cunning, don't you think?"

"What happens during the nights?" Katy asked.

"Plenty of frustration, I would imagine," Olivia laughed. "But then there's the best day to come. Very pleasant to look forward to. You report to me on the seventh day, after six days locked up, and if you're polite and ask me respectfully, I will unlock the device and release your trapped penis – just for that one day. You can wank as much as you like during that day, and most guys tell me that they do it many times, knowing that they have to report back to me again in the evening to have it locked up again for another six days."

My mind was in a whirl. Hearing this, I don't know when my cock has ever been so hard. Of course, I was unable to touch it right then, but at least it wasn't locked up and I would hopefully be able to do something about my extreme erection as soon as I got home.

What an incredible disciplinarian Olivia was!

This discussion had only served to delay the next part of my discipline for that day. I had been promised another caning and I just hoped against hope that it would be administered soon.

I found the waiting almost as unpleasant as the canings themselves. Another ten minutes in the corner passed while I thought of nothing other than the unbelievable pain that was soon coming my way courtesy of Mrs Hamilton's favourite cane.

"Right young man, we'll have you in position for your caning please." Olivia said after what seemed like an eternity of panic and anxiety.

I knew this meant we would all go over to the settee where I would bury my head right down into the cushions and stick my arse up as high as it would go, legs wide open. I'd done this on each visit and got used to the exposure and complete vulnerability.

I hadn't got used to the stinging pain, however, and I doubted that I ever would. I was finding that, in between canings, I tended to forget how much it hurt. It was only during the actual application of the punishment that I was reminded as I writhed and yelled.

Once I was in position, with my flatmate and Olivia both looking on, Katy enquired whether this was in fact the best position or whether there were others.

"That's a great position for a hard caning isn't it!" she said. "For spankings, hairbrushings etc. what do you think are the best positions for maximum pain and humiliation? Over the Knee?"

"Over the knee is certainly the best and most traditional position for a hand spanking. It's ideal also for a hard hairbrushing, a painful slippering – but not very good for the cane or the tawse. Having said that, I do deal with guys of all ages and older guys may find it difficult to get over a woman's knee. In this case, the traditional position can be achieved by the Top sitting on the bed with the sub going over her knee and resting his chest on the bed. This way his bottom is well presented for a spanking, but he is quite relaxed and can therefore concentrate on the sensations radiating from his rear! A more athletic position, but also more humiliating and revealing is the wheelbarrow position where the sub is head down between the Top's legs."

"Wheelbarrow position?" Katy enquired. I froze as I heard this incredibly humiliating position being described again.

"Yes. The sub's legs are spread wide, one each side of the Top's waist, his bottom is presented right in front of the Mistress in the middle of her lap, and his head is right down on the carpet with his hands out in front of him. It is impossible in this position for the sub to protect his bare arse if the spanking gets too intense. There's no way he can reach around and get his hands over his cheeks which are completely exposed and totally vulnerable. Also, the sub's legs are stretched wide apart, thereby parting his buttocks as well, presenting his crack and arsehole for the dominant woman to see and punish. Smacking inside the crack and round and across the hole will always produce a more vocal response from the sub!"

I stuck my bottom up and continued to wait obediently.

"What about just bending over?" Katy asked.

"Touch your toes! This is the traditional instruction for someone to be caned, tawsed or paddled. Again, an older guy may find this difficult to do and, in this case, he can be told to get his hands as far down his legs as he can. Some people feel that bending over like this stretches the cheeks too much and reduces the flesh that's ready to absorb the pain of the strokes."

"I see," Katy said thoughtfully. "What's a better way?"

"A better way is often to bend over something like the arm of a Chesterfield. This is quite low, so most men can get over it, stretch right forward and push their bottom up. This presents the bum at a much better angle, particularly if the recipient goes right over with their legs off the ground. The cane or whatever can then be applied to the lower part of his cheeks which are just crying out to be punished in this position. He'll be reminded he's been caned or punished each time he sits down!"

"You certainly know your subject Miss," Katy said appreciatively.

CHAPTER NINE – THE ULTIMATE POSITION FOR A REALLY MEMORABLE CANING.

"What we haven't done yet is put Daniel into the ultimate position for a really memorable caning," Olivia said.

I was getting increasingly anxious now, but I knew better than to question either of them. I just stuck my arse up and waited.

"What's the ultimate position?" Katy asked predictably.

"On the bed," Olivia replied. "I spread a couple of towels on the bed and then get the guy to kneel up, head right down on the sheets, bottom right up, legs wide open. It's more or less what Daniel is doing now, but it's better on the bed as he can masturbate himself while being punished. This method can either be just himself adopting this particularly humiliating position, or, if you place a few pillows or cushions on the bed, he can go over these with his tummy on the cushions and his bare bum in the air. This is an ideal position in which to get him to part his legs really wide, exposing everything, including his balls hanging down and his cock."

"About as humiliating as you can get," Katy remarked.

"Yes. If you're going to give a caning, or use the tawse, paddle, hairbrush, or even the birch, his cheeks are spread wide for punishment and his tackle is available to be teased and fondled between strokes. It may often be best to put a towel over the pillows or cushions as pre-cum may be leaking now. Some guys actually want to cum while being punished in this position and after all, that's what consenting adult male CP is supposed to be all about!"

This conversation had taken a surprising new turn.

"You're allowing him to wank?" Katy enquired tentatively.

"I said guys WANT to cum. I didn't say I let them. When guys really get into the whole mindset of submission, humiliation and obedience, I move them on to the bed. They are strictly instructed that they can stimulate their penises as much as they like as long as they don't actually cum. They can keep themselves hard, rock hard in fact usually during my canings, but they mustn't shoot their load. Continuous masturbation is allowed –

even encouraged – but without the satisfaction of a climax. If they do cum, they spend two long, frustrating weeks in chastity and then report again for their normal discipline which will be carried out on the settee until they show me they can be trusted to receive punishment and discipline on the bed again."

I was surprised and complimented by what came next.

"Tell you what," Olivia said. "Young Daniel here is doing so well. Let's all go into the bedroom now and let him experience the ultimate – punishment and stimulation together. I think he deserves it!"

I rose submissively from the couch and followed my wonderful Mistress. We all went upstairs to the bedroom where a firm double bed awaited me. The cover and duvet had been removed and two towels were already spread out on the sheet. As I might have guessed, Mrs Hamilton's apparent sudden change of heart had been no such thing. She'd had this in mind for me all along.

I climbed onto the bed, put my head right down and stuck my bare butt right up. I parted my legs as widely as I could and waited.

Just being in that position was making my cock hard. I stroked it and stuck my arse up proudly. I knew what an attractive, manly bum I had and I displayed it with pride, and of course not a little trepidation. I suspected that this was going to be my most painful caning so far and I was not wrong.

"I always cane in sixes," my Mistress announced, not telling us anything we didn't know. "For the initial six, I'm going to use my thin, whippy junior cane."

There were three canes on the bedside chest of drawers and I guessed that I was going to feel all three!

"Bottom right up!"

She began.

THWHIPP!

A lusty stroke, right across the very centre of my arse. Boy that stung!

Tap, tap, tap ... then ... THWHIPP!

A second, slightly harder stroke landed a little lower than the first.

"Ow! Please Miss!"

Tap, tap, tap, ...   then ... THWHIPP!

A much harder stroke this time.

How that little whippy cane HURT! It found a lower place still to inflict its excruciating agony. It sank deep into my soft buttocks and bounced away again, producing an impressive raised weal and a satisfying sting.

"AAAAAAAAAAAH!"

I cried loudly to no one in particular. It just came out.

I frantically masturbated in an attempt to cope that way.

The fourth stroke came without warning.

THWHACK!

Each stroke was a little lower than the previous one. This one whistled down to take me by surprise. It wrapped itself across both of my quivering buttocks equally, adding its fiery sting to the already burning furnace.

I cried, I gasped, I yelled and I pleaded, all to no avail. Olivia merely tapped again very gently, finding the next spot to punish.

"I need to go lower," she mused. "Get your bottom higher please!"

I complied and waited. What else could I do?

Now she was gently tapping right across the tender area where my bottom meets my thighs. This told me the next stroke was going to REALLY hurt!

THWHIPP!

"Aaaaaaaaaaaaaaaaaaargh!"

Having looked at this cane as Olivia had picked it up, I never would have realised its ability to inflict such intense, ferocious pain.

I clenched my buttocks tightly in the hope that this would reduce the effect of the final stroke of this six. Then I remembered this was not allowed. I quickly unclenched my bum and pushed it even further out, spreading my cheeks wide open, almost inviting that cruel cane to do its worst.

This it certainly did.

"I am going to give you the final stroke of your first six, Daniel. Remind us all what it is about the last stroke of any six that makes it particularly memorable."

"It's the hardest, Miss."

"Exactly. And therefore, the most painful. I want your bottom well presented for this one. I shan't tell you again."

THWHIPP!

"AAAAAAAAAAAAAAAAAAAAAARGH! OW! AH! OUCH! OH NO! AAAAARGH! PLEASE!"

The final stroke of my first six whistled in to complete the devastating effect by swiping hard across the same spot again. Would I ever sit down for a month?

Mrs Hamilton walked calmly over to the chest of drawers and put down the junior cane. Meanwhile, the pain it had caused spread quickly through the whole of my well-presented bottom. A thin cane like that will really penetrate deep into your butt.

Now she was picking up the next instrument of torment.

I stroked my manhood as she stroked the next cane – quite lovingly I thought.

This looked a beauty. Medium thickness, with an elegant crooked handle it was undoubtedly going to be capable of producing some searing, scorching lines of fire across my already throbbing posterior.

Mrs Hamilton touched my hairy legs and ran her hands along them, up onto my sore buttocks and into my crack. She motioned me to part my legs even wider and this I meekly did.

My legs and thighs trembled, and my two masculine cheeks, now decorated with a set of six clear red lines on each, quivered in anticipation of what was to come. I continued to masturbate gently. I had to be VERY careful in that respect! Pure terror came into my mind as I imagined the consequences.

Now the next cane was tapping itself impatiently across my outstretched arse. The torment was about to start again. I was acutely aware of the nakedness of my bottom, and the incredible stiffness of my erection.

Mrs Hamilton tapped only briefly, raised this second, new cane high and then whipped it down smartly across the very centre of my arse once again. This was a slightly stiffer, thicker cane, but still wickedly flexible. It had a devastating effect.

"Count the strokes and thank me!"

"Yes Miss."

WHACK!

"One, thank you Miss."

It lashed across my well-presented cheeks, right in the middle.

Mrs Hamilton was taking precise and careful aim. She knew exactly what she was doing. Each devastating stroke was the work of an expert, and each stroke produced a new line of intense, ferocious agony.

Immediately, Katy told me later, the desired mark of chastisement appeared, brightly glowing red, a clear line across the middle of each of my punished cheeks.

WHACK!

"Two, thank you Miss."

The vicious cane struck again, just a little lower. My two punished, provocatively displayed cheeks clenched and unclenched in a vain attempt to cope with the absolutely intolerable sting which completely possessed me.

WHACK!

"Three, thank you Miss."

The strokes were coming in a slow but sure rhythm. There was a gap of about a quarter of a minute between each, and this was not quite long enough for me to process the pain before the next one increased it.

This was Mrs Hamilton's intention. As always, she demonstrated her expert skill which had been honed to perfection through lots and lots of practice. I would love to be able to compare notes with another guy who'd been on the receiving end of her administrations. I wonder if that will ever be possible?

The superb cane was tapping again impatiently across the lowest part of my butt. I relaxed my cheeks and spread them wide open.

WHACK!

"Four, thank you Miss."

This stroke produced a strangled roar from my mouth. This stinging slash had been the hardest so far.

I started to rise, crying out "Enough! Enough Miss!" and then subsided again, knowing there was no point. There were now four rich, red weals on my bum from this thicker cane, in addition to the ones produced by the first, whippy one – four ridges evenly placed down each side. Each measured swish had produced a heartening thwhack and, for Olivia and Katy, a beautiful bounce. I had two more strokes of the second six to go.

"You're really making his bottom bounce now Miss!" Katy remarked.

"Yes. He has a beautiful bum which is a pleasure to cane," Olivia replied. "It's a joy of a behind which has a delightful way of responding to my efforts. It's smooth, full, round and just very slightly hairy - and I love the way it trembles in anticipation of each application of the rod."

My masturbation became faster and more frantic. I wasn't worried about coming as the pure terror of anticipating the next stroke was keeping me just below the boil. Wow, was I horny!

WHACK!

"Five, thank you Miss!"

Another livid line appeared, divided in the middle by my deep hairy crack. I strained to push my bottom even higher in a real effort to please my Mistress.

"That's better, Daniel!" Olivia said. "Keep it right up there for the last of this second six."

"It's about as far up as it can go Miss," I said pleadingly.

WHACK!

"Six, thank you Miss."

I'd really pushed my bottom up for that one. It increased the pain and it increased the pleasure for Olivia who admired my stamina.

That was a real, traditional, hearty stroke, applied HARD, right down low across my already swelling, ridged bottom.

Did I say it increased the pleasure for Mrs Hamilton? Well, it wasn't only pleasurable for her, I can confirm. I'd gone through the pain barrier now and into ecstasy.

Mrs Hamilton and Katy both had a good feel of my ridges and declared themselves satisfied.

Into the corner I went again, while the second cane was gently placed back on the top of the cupboard where it would quietly wait in readiness to be used again whenever necessary. I'd seen the third cane lying there in wait for me. It looked an absolute scorcher. While I stood, hands on head, cock and bum both throbbing away, Katy asked about it.

"It's my dragon cane," Olivia explained. "The best type of cane there is. Beautifully balanced, slim, smooth, dense and severe. Very expensive but worth every penny for the reaction it always produces."

I thought about this as I stood meekly waiting. In fact, I couldn't think about anything else other than Mrs Hamilton's canes. My thoughts alternated between trying to cope with the burning, scalding pain that engulfed my bottom and anticipating what the next, thicker, firmer, but still flexible dragon would feel like across my already sore cheeks.

Soon the waiting time was up and I was back on the bed with my sore, exposed, throbbing arse submissively displayed once again.

"There's no need to count these," Olivia told me. "You'll need to use all your mind power to cope with the effect this cane will produce. Ready? First stroke coming now. These are going to HURT!"

THWHACK!

With no further warning, the still supple but thicker, heavier, denser cane began its devastating work, whipping hard and low across my outstretched butt cheeks, stinging merrily and deeply into each of my already sore buttocks.

"Aaaaaaaaaaaaaaaaaaaaaaaaaaaaaaaargh! Fuck! Oh shit!"

The expletives came out of my mouth involuntarily, completely without thinking. Oh No! I immediately panicked. What would Olivia say or do? Surely, she couldn't punish me more? Thankfully, she made no response. She merely gave encouragement.

"Cry out as much as you like during these," she said. "You'll find it a complete release of tension. And don't forget to concentrate on the reason you're having this particular caning – which is?"

"It's for my general laziness and lack of application Miss."

"Absolutely. Keep in mind that this is to teach you not to be lazy and to apply yourself fully to tasks you have to complete."

"Yes Miss."

Katy spoke up brightly. "Just like you always apply yourself fully to giving your canings, don't you Miss?"

Olivia Hamilton chuckled but didn't reply. She was lining up the third, most effective cane very low down, right across my crease. She was tapping gently there for quite a while until

THWHACK!

Again, I cried out in an involuntary strangulated yell as the pain consumed and engulfed me. I squirmed and wriggled, shaking my bum to try to assuage the burning torment, but of course I couldn't. Olivia was such an expert!

"Think about your laziness again, now, please. Are you going to be lazy again?"

THWHACK!

Aaaaaaaaaaaaaaaaaaaaaaaaaaaaaaaaaaargh! No Miss! Never Miss! Never lazy again Miss!"

"Good. I'm very pleased to hear it. Let's have your bottom a little higher still, now. Right UP, as high as it will go! These next three strokes will punish you for your general lack of application. Hopefully, for your sake they will be the last three this evening. I wouldn't want to have to award extras for any reason so I would advise you to keep very still and stay obediently in position no matter how much they hurt."

"Yes Miss."

"Come around to the other side of the bed, Katy," Olivia was saying. "You can get a closer look there – a grandstand view of the proceedings!"

"Some beautiful, vivid lines – and so even," Katy replied.

Katy moved closer, I raised my bottom even higher, and Olivia swished the cane through the air. Then, without warning

THWHACK!

I cried. I yelled. I pleaded. All, of course to no avail.

THWHACK!

That one was a beauty. A lusty, heartening stroke that resonated around the room as it sank deep into my bare bum (apparently producing the most delightful bounce as Katy told me later).

As the cruel cane remorselessly did its necessary work, I squealed, gasped and yelled while Olivia concentrated on the important task in hand and Katy grinned in delight.

When it came to the last stroke, Olivia didn't disappoint.

All five of these recent strokes had been applied with increasing severity to the part of me designed for that purpose. Now all I had to do was get through the last one and I would be home and dry for tonight. She had a further explanation to give.

"In the interests of achieving maximum effect, I want you to hold your buttocks apart for me with your hands," she said. "Just stretch your bum a little wider open so that my cane can sting the parts no cane usually reaches."

I couldn't believe what I was hearing. Just when I thought I was nearly through, this extra indignity was being imposed. I did as she said. I didn't question her, I didn't protest, I merely complied.

I felt a soothing surge of cool air deep in my crack as my arsehole was exposed even more clearly to the two females watching me.

Tap, tap, tap, then

THWHACK!

This final stroke across the centre of my presented bottom and into my open crack seemed to have the strength of all the seventeen previous strokes combined. It stung really viciously across both of my scalded, sore buttocks and, as I was pulling my cheeks so wide open for my Mistress, it stung quite a bit of the softer flesh inside my cheeks.

"Keep pulling your cheeks apart for me please Daniel," Olivia was saying.

I obeyed, not realising what she was going to do.

Suddenly she whipped that cruel, flexible, thicker, denser, even more severe DRAGON cane vertically DOWN my crack, aiming the tip to land right ON my exposed arse hole. Now that DOES hurt! It hurts more than I could possibly describe.

I uttered a blood-curdling yell, gasped, gurgled, wailed and then subsided, panting and lightly sobbing.

I felt really well punished and, for the first time ever, I felt I'd paid for my mistakes. I'd paid for my rudeness, I'd paid for the way I treated my poor wife, and I'd paid for my laziness. The vicious stinging sensations in my rear would be with me for a long time to come, and they would be a constant reminder to me to apply myself properly to tasks I had to complete.

How well a thorough caning works.

As my tears welled and flowed, my Mistress was saying "Well done, young man. A lesson well learned I would think."

"Yes Miss. Very much so, Miss. Thank you Miss."

I'd been breathing very heavily, literally gasping for breath at times. Now, finally, I relaxed and started to feel rather pleased with myself for what I'd been able to take. My torment was over.

Then she said "Well, we've just got the matter of your bad language to deal with and then that will hopefully be all for tonight!"

WHAT!

Could I have heard her right? I started to say

"But Miss ..." and then quickly stopped myself. I immediately changed this to "Yes Miss" and waited dolefully for further instructions. How could I have been so stupid firstly to swear, and secondly to think that she would overlook this lack of manners?

"Stay in position," she said forcefully. "Young men who come to me to be disciplined often think they can use bad language in my presence. They quickly learn this is not the case – as you will now. Bottom up again! I think just two more minutes with the hairbrush will be appropriate here. Time it for me, will you Katy?"

Mrs Hamilton picked up the smooth, hard wooden-backed hairbrush and set to work with it, reminding me as she smacked merrily away with increasing venom that I am always to be polite to her. By the time around twenty more viciously stinging smacks had been applied vigorously to my upturned striped, burning bottom, I would have been ready to agree to anything – absolutely anything – if she would only stop relentlessly spanking me with that terrible little brush.

After what was only about two minutes, but seemed like an eternity, the smacking stopped – but the burning continued. Would it ever cease?

Would I ever be able to place my poor, punished bottom onto a chair again? The intense throbbing in my rear seemed to still be increasing as she told me to get up.

Wiping my eyes, I struggled off the bed and onto my feet.

"Pants and trousers back on," she said brightly.

"Thank you, Miss," I said, bending down to put on my pants, which I carefully and slowly pulled up over my scalded swollen cheeks.

"I remind you that I will not tolerate bad language. You are here to learn and to take whatever discipline I decide is called for."

"Yes Miss. Thank you Miss."

She put down the smooth, particularly painful hairbrush and said firmly

"Remember my hairbrush is always here to provide extra punishments if needed. It's always near at hand and it is a very easy little additional method I frequently use when I think a young man has not learnt complete compliance and humility. Two minutes with this seem like an eternity, don't they?"

"Yes Miss."

Katy was looking straight at me and grinning. Then she turned to Olivia and said "You know so much about discipline Miss. I just wonder if there's anything at all that you don't know."

"Try me."

"Well Miss, supposing I got into this myself? Supposing I did discipline sessions with a partner ... er ... what do people usually do afterwards?"

"Well of course, that's entirely up to you. Many people are so turned-on, they have sex right away, or at least, the guy frantically masturbates. Others go completely the opposite way and the sub is put immediately into chastity. He will most likely be feeling extremely horny and desperate for relief. An ideal time, therefore, for the Top to produce a male chastity device for the sub to obediently put on while his Mistress watches, key in hand."

Mrs Hamilton had a thing about chastity!

I struggled to get into my trousers and pull them up as I heard this. I couldn't imagine the terror I would feel if Olivia decided to put me into chastity right then. I didn't look at either of them as she continued...

"It can be really difficult to get the sub's cock soft enough to go into the tube when he's got such a raging hard-on. However, perseverance is all that is necessary, and a little patience. Maybe a couple of ice cubes. Eventually the erection will subside enough for the cock to be locked into place and then of course it can no longer even be touched, let alone masturbated. The Mistress keeps the key, and the sub goes home frustrated beyond belief. A man's balls are producing semen all the time and the sub's balls will be particularly full at this time, immediately his punishment is over."

"Yes, I'm sure," Katy agreed, obviously acutely aware of the heaviness of MY balls right then.

"If the sub's bottom is hot and throbbing, this will, over time, cause the production of even more semen which of course will have nowhere to go if relief can't be had. Quite a difficult night is awaiting the sub who will find himself absolutely desperate for relief when he wakes at 2.00 am with his cock pressing urgently into the hard encasing of the penis tube that encloses it, pointing firmly down. The device will not only prevent masturbation, but will also prevent an erection. Frustration that can be completely mind-blowing!"

"Wow!" was all that Katy could say, adding "What can a man do?"

"There's no way out. You have to get through the night as best you can and then hope against hope that your Mistress will agree to release you in the morning, or at least some time the next day. A second night will obviously be even more difficult because, as I said, even more sperm will have been produced in the balls by then and the effect is cumulative ... as one of my subs told me when he reported back to me in chastity on the third day he'd had his cock locked up. The look of pleading and pure desperation on his face will always stay with me."

"Wow! What did you do?" Katy asked in wonderment.

"Well, when I said I hadn't yet decided when I was going to release him, he got down on his knees in front of me and begged. I made a cup of tea and slowly drank it while I thought about his predicament. I then told him to stand up and stand to attention. After five minutes or so, while I made a couple of phone calls, I told him to put his coat on and go home, instructing him to report back to me again the next day at the same time when I would say whether or not he would be released. They don't call me Mistress for nothing!"

"You must be the best Mistress any guy has ever had," Katy said.

Olivia didn't acknowledge this compliment, merely continuing with her account of the young man in chastity.

"Imagine his feelings as he left me, and imagine his torment in the middle of that extra night. Imagine not knowing, when he reported back yet again the following day, whether he would be released then or have to wait longer. That's what I call real adult discipline!"

I decided then and there, never to displease Olivia in any way at all if I could possibly help it.

"Time to go, young man," she said quite kindly. "We've dealt with three things over these first three visits. Your rudeness, the way you treated your wife, plus your laziness and general lack of application."

"Yes Miss."

"The final caning today, with the dragon cane, is the most severe discipline I give. You've experienced that now and need to know that it is not normally used. Your future, regular visits will consist of what I call a standard tariff of spankings, bottom canings, hand canings, etc. These methods will work well to keep you on the straight and narrow path. If there are any particular transgressions you feel you need to report to me, they will be dealt with by additional treatments that may well include the dragon cane or even the birch. This way, altogether, you will grow in confidence, and learn COMPLETE humility, which is what I always achieve with all my pupils. You have a magnificent set of buttocks and it is an absolute pleasure dealing with them, young man."

I blushed at this compliment, only to hear more terrifying punishment methods being described. Methods that seemed likely to be used on me.

"Have you ever had an enema, Daniel?"

"No Miss. I'm not even quite sure what that is, Miss."

"Then may I suggest you look it up on the internet when you get home, young man. Suffice to say, a tube is involved along with a large quantity of warm soapy water. Quite embarrassing for a grown but naughty man."

I couldn't speak at all at the thought of exactly what this incredible humiliation would involve.

"Do you have anything to say?"

I considered several things I COULD say in the circumstances, but perhaps you won't be surprised to learn what I DID, in fact, say.

"I only want to say thank you Miss. Thank you very much for disciplining me Miss. I've learned a lot already and I'm very grateful."

"Good man. I know you are. See you next Tuesday. We won't say now what is in store for you then, except that I shall take you to the next level of both discipline and submission."

"Yes Miss. Thank you Miss."

THE END

Would YOU be able to receive discipline at that kind of level – and then THANK your disciplinarian? Think about that – and then read some of the other excellent, superb adult discipline books by Mark Maguire and Mistress Jade.